Thanksgiving by the Sea

A Haunting by the Sea Mystery

by

Kathi Daley

Haunting by the Sea

Homecoming by the Sea
Secrets by the Sea
Missing by the Sea
Betrayal by the Sea
Thanksgiving by the Sea

Chapter 1

Friday, November 16

You know what they say about the best-laid plans?

I was on my way to a weekend getaway with Trevor Johnson, one of my two best friends, when I got a call from Officer Woody Baker. Woody was a good guy who'd helped me out on more than one occasion, so when he asked for my help in tracking down the man who'd shot a local social worker, I didn't feel I could turn him down in spite of the fact that Trevor and I were still trying to recover from the worst cruise in history. Well, maybe not the worst in history; I did remember the Titanic. But while our cruise may not have been quite as bad as that history-making cruise gone wrong, it definitely wasn't the relaxing time I'd been promised by my other best friend, Mackenzie Reynolds, and her new guy friend, Ty Matthews. Not only had I run into a ghost on my second night aboard, but the ship had been hijacked, and other passengers had ended up dead before the nightmare at sea was over as well.

"My name is Amanda Parker. Officer Baker sent me," I said to the woman at the front desk of the hospital. "I'm here to meet Carmen Rosewood."

The woman looked down at her log. "Yes. Ms. Rosewood is waiting for you. Just take the elevator to the second floor and then make a left. Trinity Rosewood is in room 202."

Offering the woman a look of thanks, I headed toward the elevator. I really doubted, due to the unique circumstance, that I'd be able to help Woody accomplish what he hoped, but I knew I needed to try.

"Carmen Rosewood?" I asked the dark-haired woman sitting next to the hospital bed currently occupied by Trinity Rosewood.

"Yes." The woman nodded. "You must be Amanda Parker."

"I am. I'm sorry about your sister."

A tear rolled down the woman's face. "Who would do this to Trinity? She's a good person who spent her life helping others. This whole thing makes no sense."

I offered the woman a gentle smile. "I know. I'm sorry." I glanced at the woman currently hooked up to a variety of monitors and machines. "Has there been any change?"

Carmen slowly shook her head. "According to the doctor, all we can do is wait. Either Trinity will fight to live or she won't. There really isn't anything more the doctors can do at this point."

"I've never had the pleasure of meeting Trinity, but Woody assures me she is a fighter."

Carmen offered me a tiny smile. "She is. If anyone can survive this, it will be Trinity." She glanced away from her sister and toward me. "I'm not sure why Officer Baker wanted you to spend time with Trinity, but he asked me to allow you to sit with her for a while, and I agreed." She stood up. "If you are some sort of a psychic or healer, please do everything you can. I'll be in the waiting room. You can just come and get me when you are finished."

"Thank you. I won't be long."

Sitting in the chair Carmen had just vacated, I realized all I could do at this point was to open my mind and wait. Woody is a fantastic cop who doesn't normally need help to do his job, but the shooting in question took place after dark in the driveway of the woman's home, and no one had seen who'd pulled the trigger except for the woman herself. The problem was that Trinity was in a coma and couldn't tell anyone what had happened. Given the fact that I could see and speak to ghosts, Woody hoped I might be able to communicate with her. I agreed to try, but ghosts were dead, and this woman was simply unconscious, so I really doubted it would work.

"Trinity. Are you here?" I asked in a gentle voice. "Can you hear me?"

There was no response. I looked at the monitors which seemed to be beeping along steadily. Trinity looked to be at peace. She didn't appear to be close to death. I honestly doubted that I would be able to connect with her. Deciding to see if my alter ego Alyson was around, I silently called out to her. She appeared.

"Can you sense her?" I asked in a quiet voice.

"No," the half of me that existed in spirit form replied. "The woman is still very much alive. Her essence has not separated from her body. I guess that is a good thing, but I'm not sure there is a lot you and I can do at this point."

I nodded. "I thought as much, but I had to try. I'm going to wait here for a few minutes just in case we're wrong and Trinity is trying to reach out to us."

Alyson disappeared, and I reached out and took the woman's hand in my own. "My name is Amanda. I'm not sure if you can hear me, but if you can, I'm here to help you. I can't stay long, but I will be back tomorrow. If you can find a way to communicate with me, I want you to know that you don't have to be afraid of me. I only want to help."

Trinity didn't move, but I sensed that my message had been received. I stood and walked out into the waiting room.

"So?" Carmen asked.

"Your sister is at peace. She is strong. I didn't sense distress. I wasn't able to speak with her directly today, so I'd like to come back tomorrow. Honestly, I'm not sure I can do anything to help Trinity, but I'd like to try."

"Yes. Of course. Please feel free to come back any time. Officer Baker didn't go into any detail, but he did say that you have a unique gift and might be able to help."

"I'll do what I can."

Once I returned to my car, I called Woody from my cell.

"Well?" he asked.

"Trinity is very much alive and is not even close to separating from her spirit. I do plan to return tomorrow and try again, but at this point, I think we are going to need another way to identify the person who shot her."

I could hear Woody breathing, but he didn't answer right away. Eventually, he spoke. "Yeah. I've been working on it, but I'm not really getting anywhere. I don't suppose you'd like to grab some lunch and we could talk it through. At this point, I feel like I've hit a dead end."

"I'd be happy to talk it through with you. I'll grab some sandwiches and meet you at your office. We can eat and chat in the conference room where we won't be interrupted or overheard."

"Great. And thank you."

"Anytime."

Once I hung up with Woody, I called Trevor.

"Any luck?" he asked.

"No, but given the fact that I can see and speak to ghosts, that is a good thing. Alyson seemed to feel that at this point, the woman is well connected to her spirit. I'm going to head over and chat with Woody about the case. Do you want to come?"

"Yeah. I'd like that. Do you want to meet at Woody's office?"

"That would be great. I'm going to pick up some sandwiches. I should be there in twenty minutes or so."

After I hung up with Trevor, I headed toward the deli. After our cruise from hell ended early, Trevor and I had decided to spend a few days touring the San Juan Islands while Mac and Ty went off on their own romantic holiday. Trevor and I had been skirting the *friends* versus *something more than friends* issue for a while now, and I was sorry we hadn't had the chance to really explore our options. Not that I would have considered turning Woody down when he'd asked for my help, but it did seem that Trevor and I were destined to remain in the friend zone for all eternity. And maybe that was a good thing. Maybe taking our relationship to the next level would end in disaster. Trevor had been one of my best friends, along with Mac, since I'd first moved to Cutter's Cove as a teenager in witness protection. He meant a lot to me. More than I'd even realized until I'd returned to Cutter's Cove ten years after having left when witness protection ended. Was I really willing to risk that friendship by exploring a romance? I knew deep in my heart that once you crossed the line between friendship and romance, you could never really go back.

"Two Italian subs and a veggie sub," I said to the man behind the counter at the deli.

"Coming right up."

Walking over to the cooler, I grabbed three sodas. The place was pretty deserted today, but I supposed it was because it was a weekday during the off-season when the town as a whole tended to be somewhat deserted.

"Chips?" the man asked.

"No. Just the sandwiches and these sodas." I picked up the regional newspaper and an image of a man being shot flashed into my mind. Okay, that was odd. My superpower seemed to be to see and speak to ghosts so I could help them do whatever it was they needed to do to move on. I didn't have premonitions. At least I hadn't until now if that is even what was going on. Of course, I'd had prophetic dreams in the past. I supposed that flashes of insight were really nothing more than an extension of that. "I'll take this newspaper as well," I added.

Once I paid the man, I headed toward Woody's office. Trevor's truck was already there.

"I hope Italian subs are okay," I offered a sandwich and soda to each man.

"Sounds perfect to me," Woody replied. "Are Mac and Ty coming as well?"

"They are currently sequestered away at an undisclosed location getting their romance on," Trevor said.

"We can call or text if we need them, but let's only bother them if we really need their help," I suggested.

"Sounds fine to me," Woody said as he opened his soda. "I really want to thank the two of you for dropping everything to help out."

"We're always happy to do what we can." I opened the paper and turned to page two. I laid the paper on the table and pointed to a photo of a tall man dressed in a dark suit. "What can you tell me about this man?"

Woody looked at the photo. "His name is Bryson Teller. He is an attorney specializing in family law and child custody. Why do you ask?"

"While I was at the deli, I picked up the newspaper and had a flash of this man being shot."

Woody raised a brow. "Do you think it was a premonition?"

"I honestly don't know. I have had prophetic dreams in the past, but nothing like this. Whatever happened, if anything actually happened, is brand new. Still, given everything else, I do think we might want to take my flash seriously."

"I'll call him," Woody offered.

Trevor and I waited while Woody looked up and then dialed the law office where the man worked. He was told that Bryson was in court, so he left a message.

"I'm not sure what more I can do at this point," he said after hanging up.

"Where did the shooting take place?" Trevor asked.

Furrowing my brow, I answered. "I'm not sure. The whole thing really caught me off guard, and I didn't really pay much attention to the details. If it happens again, I'll be ready, and I'll try to notice the details." I opened my soda. "Would Trinity and Bryson have worked together on the same cases?"

"Sure," Woody said. "As a social worker, Trinity's job is to do whatever is in the best interest of the individuals in her care. Sometimes that means prosecuting others who wish to do harm to those she has been entrusted to protect, whether it be children, the elderly, or those who are unable to act as an advocate for themselves."

"I think we should take this flash seriously, especially given what happened to Trinity," I said. "I know the man is in court, but there must be a way to get a message to him."

"I can try," Woody said. "I'm just not sure what to say. *My friend had a premonition that you might be shot at some unknown time in some unknown location* probably isn't going to cut it."

"Yeah. I guess we do need more information. Let's see if we can find any current cases that Trinity and Bryson were working on together," I suggested.

Woody stood up. "I'm going to go into my office and make a few calls. I won't be long if the two of you don't mind waiting."

I glanced at Trevor. He shrugged.

"Okay," I said. "We can wait."

Woody picked up his sandwich and his soda and headed back toward his office.

"I'm really sorry about this," I said to Trevor. "Tracking down the person who shot a social worker in her driveway is not the relaxing getaway we talked about."

"It's not a problem at all," Trevor said. "If there is anything either of us can do to help Woody out, I think it is important to do so. It did occur to me that we might fit in some relaxation around helping Woody."

I leaned in just a bit. "Oh. What did you have in mind?"

"I have a new recipe I've been wanting to try out. If you don't mind being a guinea pig, I thought we could have dinner at my place."

"Well, I'm not sure how I feel about the guinea pig part, but I'm game. I'm sure whatever you make will be delicious. Are you still planning to take the weekend off?"

"I am since I'd already planned to be off, and it is a slow time of the year, I figured we'd do what we could to help Woody but maybe work in some fun as well. There is a pub that recently opened down the coast that I've been wanting to try out. If we have time, maybe we can take a drive."

"Sounds fun." I looked up when Woody returned to the room. "Well?"

"Based on the conversation I had with Bryson's assistant, he has three cases he is working on with Trinity. One case is a child custody case involving the maternal grandfather of seven-year-old twins and their stepdad. The biological mother named her husband as guardian of her daughters should anything happen to her, but apparently the woman's father, the grandfather of the twins, is suing for custody."

"And the biological father?" I asked.

"As far as I can tell, he is not now nor has he ever been in the picture, but I only received a brief summary and am waiting for more details about the case."

"Okay, what else are they working on?" I asked.

"Trinity was working on a neglect case involving four children aged ten and under who were left alone much of the time while the parents were working or otherwise occupied. Apparently, she has tried working with the parents to rectify the situation, but two weeks ago, the oldest was trying to cook dinner for his siblings and set fire to the kitchen. Trinity and Bryson worked together to have the children removed from the home. The father was arrested after he picked them up from school without permission with the intent of taking them to stay with his brother who lives in Utah. It's a pretty big mess."

"Sounds volatile enough to lead to someone going over the deep end. And the third one?" I asked.

"The third case involves a fifteen-year-old boy named Devon Long, who has been in the foster care system since he was four. Both of his parents were sent to prison for armed robbery. The boy's mother was released from prison early due to overcrowding and for good behavior. She has petitioned to have her son returned to her, but the foster parents are balking. When they accepted the child into their home for such a long-term assignment, they were concerned about becoming too attached, but they were told the boy's parents would be in prison until after he turned eighteen, so having him returned to either parent wouldn't be an issue."

"And now it is an issue."

"Exactly."

"So what is the plan at this point?" I asked.

"I'm going to speak to all three parties, and I plan to track Bryson down and speak to him personally. He is going to be in court until four, so I plan to catch up with him there."

Wadding up my sandwich wrapper, I tossed it in the trash. "Okay. It sounds as if you have that handled. I'm going to go by the hospital again tomorrow and try to connect with Trinity. I don't have high hopes that I will be able to, but I'm willing to try. In the meantime, if you need anything, call or text. I'll be around, but I may not be home, so just call my cell."

"I will, and thanks again. I'll let you know how my interviews with the three people of interest go. When it comes to child custody, there is always the potential for a peaceful negotiation to turn volatile."

I stood up to leave when an image flashed through my mind. "I had another image," I said aloud. "It was the same man I'd seen before being shot again, but this time I noticed the setting. He was standing on the stairs in front of the courthouse."

Woody frowned. "Maybe I'd better head over there now."

"Yeah. I think you should. This image was different than the last one. This one felt as if I was seeing it in real-time."

The woman who manned the front poked her head in through the door of the conference room where we were still talking. "There has been a shooting at the courthouse. A man is dead. All units in the area have been dispatched to respond."

Woody grabbed his vest and his gun. "I'm on my way."

Chapter 2

"Can you believe we were in Seattle this morning getting ready to rent a car and head to the San Juan Islands?" Trevor asked after we'd shared the wonderful meal he'd prepared, and had settled onto his back deck which was located right on the beach.

"That was this morning?" I laid my head on Trevor's shoulder. We were sitting in a lounger for two. It was a cool night, but between the fire in the pit and the warm blanket he'd wrapped around us, it felt just right.

"Really early this morning," he clarified, "but this morning all the same. This has really been a crazy week. Can you believe it was only five days ago that we were boarding the ship for what we thought would be a weeklong luxury cruise?"

"It does seem like a lot longer than five days. In that past five days, we've solved two murders, brought down a swindler who'd bilked people out of millions of dollars, been lost at sea, and saved a whole lot of lives. I would say that it was a really bad week, but this seems sort of perfect."

"It does," he agreed.

"I just hope we can figure out who put Trinity in a coma and gunned down Bryson on the courthouse steps. It seems unreal to me that a man could be gunned down in broad daylight and no one saw what happened."

"Woody said that Bryson was shot by a sniper from a distance."

I tried to relax as I focused my attention on the moon shining down on the calm sea. The waves, which at times crashed onto the shore, were gentle rollers this evening. "Do you think that's odd?" I asked after a minute. "The person who shot Trinity shot her with a handgun from a fairly close range, but her injury wasn't fatal, whereas Bryson was shot with a sniper rifle from a distance, possibly a long distance, and yet the bullet hit him square in the chest. I know logic would dictate that if a family law attorney and a social worker who were working together were both shot within twenty-four hours, their shootings would have been carried out by the same person, but were they?"

Trevor turned his head slightly. "Do you think there were two different shooters?"

I hesitated. "I'm not sure. Maybe. I know that the channel five news team announced that the two shootings are related and that the authorities are looking for a single shooter, but I'm not convinced that it is as cut and dried as that."

"The pair did take on some pretty emotional cases," Trevor reminded me. "It does make sense that the shootings were the result of one of the cases they were working on together."

"Maybe."

"I know Bryson's ghost wasn't hanging around when we showed up today, but do you think it is worth going back for a second look?" Trevor asked.

I exhaled slowly. "I don't know. Maybe. I guess it wouldn't hurt to go back to the courthouse tomorrow and see if his spirit is lurking about, but my sense is that he'd already moved on before we even arrived. Not all spirits linger."

"I know. And maybe the guy didn't have any unfinished business. Most people don't."

Turning my body slightly, I draped my legs over Trevor's. It really was nice sitting out here when the beach was completely deserted. I really did want to do what I could to figure out who had shot two pretty awesome people, but at this moment, I really just wanted to allow my mind and my emotions to rest. I would go back by the hospital tomorrow and try to connect with Trinity if she hadn't yet woken, and I'd go back to the courthouse and make sure that Bryson wasn't lurking about, and I'd meet with Woody and try to talk through all the possible angles, but right now, I just wanted to connect to the quiet corner of my mind where serenity and contentment lived.

"This is really nice," I said after a moment of silence. "I bet you must sit out here all the time."

"Not as often as you might think. I work a lot of evenings, and when I am home, I tend to putter around in my workshop. I've been working on the desk Mac wants, and I'm close to being done. I'd love to give it to her for Christmas."

Lifting my head slightly. "Christmas?"

"It is only five and a half weeks away, and the last two of those are always so busy with the Christmas Carnival, so I figure I should get my projects done before it starts."

"Wow. You're right. Christmas really is just around the corner. It really snuck up on me." I paused to remember the last time I'd been in Cutter's Cove for Christmas. It had been ten years ago, and I'd almost died when the Ferris wheel I was riding on malfunctioned. Actually, it hadn't malfunctioned, it had been tampered with, but that was a whole other murder mystery I really didn't want to focus on. "Remember the sleigh ride you, Mac, and I took?"

"I do. That evening, like this one, was pretty cozy with us all wrapped up in the blanket."

"I used to think about that evening after I went home to New York," I said.

Trevor kissed the top of my head, which was resting on his chest. "Yeah. Me too. Often. After you left, things weren't the same, and after Mac left, things were downright depressing. I really missed us. I missed the friendship we shared and the crazy adventures we continually found ourselves involved in."

"Like that treasure hunt that one Thanksgiving?" I asked.

"Exactly like that."

I smiled at the memory. "It is going to mean a lot that we are all going to be together again this Thanksgiving," I said. "Mac and Ty will be back on Monday or Tuesday of next week. My mom is planning a huge meal on Thursday. She invited a friend, so that will make six of us. I think I'll invite Woody as well. He may have plans, or he may have to work, but if he isn't busy, I want to be sure he has somewhere to go."

"I'm kind of surprised Avery didn't come along with your mother."

Avery Kinkaid is a young woman whose life we'd saved around Halloween. She'd needed to hide out, so I'd sent her to live with my mother in New York.

"Mom said Avery is all settled into the house in New York. I think she was happy to stay behind, and my mom really wanted to be here with us, so it all seemed to work out."

"That's good. I was worried about how she would adjust."

"She went through something pretty traumatic, but she is a survivor." I traced a finger over Trevor's chest. "I was thinking of taking a run tomorrow before I head to the hospital. If you want to come along, I can go slow and take it easy on you."

"I'd love to come, and I've seen you run, so yes, I will need you to be gentle with me."

I laughed. "We can bring the dogs. I always run slowly when I have Tucker with me."

Tucker was my twelve-year-old German Shepard. I also had a young golden retriever named Sunny.

"The trail along the shore isn't too crowded this time of the year," Trevor pointed out.

"That sounds nice. My body feels tight after being confined this past week. I really need to work out some of the kinks."

Trevor tightened his arms around my body. I imagined he was thinking about working out kinks. Suddenly I was as well. I tilted my head slightly, so I was looking up at him. He opened his mouth as if he was going to say something, but instead, he lowered his head and touched his lips gently to mine. If I'd been in charge of my reaction, I might have pulled back and stopped to analyze things, but at that moment, all thoughts flew from my mind, and the only thing I was aware of was his lips on mine. He deepened the kiss once I'd responded to his first tentative exploration and all thoughts of seaside runs and working out sore muscles were pushed to the back of my mind.

Chapter 3

Saturday, November 17

I woke with a smile. I'd been tempted to let the makeout session Trevor had instigated the previous evening progress to its natural conclusion, but there was a lot at stake, and in the end, I'd chickened out and claimed fatigue. Trevor had brought me home and dropped me off. He left me with a gentle kiss and a promise to be here at seven, so we could go running before the weekend joggers claimed the trails. I turned my head and looked at the clock. It was already six-fifteen. No time to lay about and daydream about the perfect ending to our dinner last night.

Leaning up onto my elbows, I looked at the menagerie on my bed. My dog, Tucker, laid next to me while my dog, Sunny, covered my feet. Shadow, my ghost seeing cat, was curled up on the extra pillow next to my head. "Are you ready to get up?"

Tucker and Sunny wagged their tails as if to convey that yes they were ready to rise for the day, but Shadow just yawned and scowled, then lowered his head and went back to sleep.

Twisting, I turned my body so that I was able to slide my legs to the side in spite of all the obstacles. Planting my feet on the floor, I slid out of bed, grabbing my robe from the chair as I did so. The dogs jumped down onto the floor after they realized we actually were getting up. I shuffled across the room and into the attached bathroom. Once I'd brushed my teeth, washed up, and put my hair into a ponytail, I headed back into the bedroom to find a clean running suit. Grabbing my running shoes, I headed downstairs.

"You're up early," Mom said. "After your weeklong drama, I figured you'd sleep in."

Pouring a cup of coffee, I turned toward Mom. "Trevor is coming over. We're going running." I glanced at Tucker, who seemed to be walking extra slowly this morning. "Actually maybe walking. We'll let Tucker decide."

"I think the drop in temperature is messing with his joints. The poor guy has seemed stiff all week."

"We'll take it easy on him. If the sand along the beach trail is too soft, we'll move onto the hard-packed jogging path."

"It does look like it is going to be a beautiful day. Cold, but not a cloud in the sky. How was your dinner last night?"

Sitting at the table, I began putting on my shoes. "Excellent. Trevor made this sauce with spicy sausage in a cream base. It was fantastic."

"I'll have to get the recipe. Trevor has come up with quite a few recipes that have turned out to be some of my favorites."

I grinned. "He really is amazing."

Mom smiled back. "Yes, he is. Do the two of you have plans today after you finish your run or walk as the case may be?"

"I want to go over to the hospital and try to connect with Trinity again. After that, I'm going to head to the courthouse to make sure the man who was killed yesterday isn't still lurking around. And once I have accomplished both of those tasks, I thought I'll check in with Woody. If there is time left, Trevor and I talked about taking a drive down the coast."

"Sounds like a full day. Should I assume you won't be home for dinner?"

I thought about Trevor's lips on mine. Dinner with my mom would be the safe bet. "No, we'll either eat out or make something over at Trevor's. Are you still planning to have your friend over? What is his name? Steve? Or is it Mike?"

"It's Carson, and yes, I do still plan to have him over this evening."

"I do want to meet him. Maybe next week." I glanced at the clock. "Trevor should be here any minute. I need to go and grab my sweatshirt."

By the time I got back downstairs, Trevor had arrived. He chatted with my mom for a few minutes, and then we headed toward the beach trail with the dogs.

"I think we may need to walk instead of run," I said as we headed toward the bluff. "Tucker is having a tough time this morning."

"No problem. It is less likely that you will embarrass me with your superior fitness level if we walk."

I put my hand on Trevor's muscular arm. "I don't know. You feel pretty fit to me."

Trevor winked but didn't reply.

"Our discussion about Christmas last night got me thinking about all the things I want to be sure to do. When I lived here before, you, Mac, and I cut down our own trees. I think it would be fun to do that again this year."

"I agree," Trevor answered. "Let me know when you want to go, and I'll arrange to take the day off."

"You're closed on Mondays anyway, and I can go whenever, so let's plan on the Monday after Thanksgiving if that works for Mac. We can ask her when she gets back from her romantic getaway."

"Sounds good." Trevor wove his fingers through mine. "So I learned something interesting on my way over to your place this morning."

"Oh, and what's that?" I asked.

"I stopped for gas and ran into a buddy of mine who works for the district attorney's office. He let it slip that his office is looking at Bryson Teller's wife as possibly being responsible for his death."

I had to admit I wasn't expecting that. "Really? Why?"

"I guess the couple had been having problems and according to my buddy, Bryson had recently moved out of the home he shared with his wife, and she had recently consulted a divorce attorney."

"So if she planned to divorce the guy, why kill him?"

"I don't know. My friend didn't know. And when I brought up the fact that the guy was killed with a round fired from a sniper rifle, he admitted that the way the bullet was delivered made it less likely that the wife was the shooter, but it was still possible that she'd hired someone."

"I suppose, but it seems like a longshot unless there are some extenuating circumstances we don't know about."

"I agree. Still, if the DA is spending time looking at the wife, he must have a reason for doing so."

"True." I reached down, picked up a stick, and tossed it for Sunny. "And if the DA is looking at the wife, then he must not think the death of the attorney and the social worker are related."

"It's hard to say. The shooting just happened yesterday afternoon, so the DA's office really hasn't had time to look into much of anything. My guess is that there is an apparent and obvious reason to consider the wife as a suspect. I suppose the details will eventually come out. Maybe Woody knows."

"We can ask him when we stop by later. Are you are still planning to come with me to the hospital, courthouse, and Woody's office?"

"Wherever you go, I will follow," Trevor said, gallantly bowing as he did so.

I rolled my eyes. "Oh, please. The charming prince bit isn't going to fly. I've seen you blow soda through your nose."

"When we were in high school," he defended. "I haven't done that in over a year, maybe two."

I laughed and kissed him on the cheek. "Should we turn around?"

"We should if we want to accomplish everything on your list. If you want to change out of your running clothes, I can hang out with your mom while you clean up, and then we can drive to my place so I can shower and change. I suppose we can head to the hospital to visit with Trinity first and then take it from there."

"That sounds like a good plan. Let's stop and get some flowers on the way to the hospital. I know Trinity is in a coma and won't even know the flowers are there, but it still feels like the right thing to do."

"There is a florist next door to the hospital. Should we eat while we're out?"

I nodded. "Yeah, we can grab something along the way. I've been wanting one of those shrimp sandwiches they sell out on the pier. Maybe we can stop and get one after we visit the hospital but before we go by the courthouse or talk to Woody."

"Sounds fine to me, but perhaps we should call Woody and make sure he doesn't have an update before we go running all over town."

Chapter 4

When Trevor and I arrived at the hospital, no one was in Trinity's room other than Trinity. Woody had cleared it with the hospital for me to spend some time with her, but not for Trevor, so he agreed to hang out in the waiting room. As I had the previous day, I sat down in the chair next to the bed. I gently placed my hand over Trinity's and then closed my eyes and tried to connect with her essence. As I'd already told Woody, I'd never connected with a living person before in quite this manner, so I had no expectation that I would today, but I figured there was no harm in trying.

Slowly taking in a breath, I calmed my mind. I tried to create a space for Trinity to enter should she wish to. The steady beep, beep, beep of the heart monitor was audible beyond the emptiness I'd sought to create. I focused my mind on the woman whose hand I touched. I listened for a sound, a word, or the gentlest of whispers. Sometimes those I was meant to help come to me in a grand manner, while other times the only hint of their presence was a feeling in my gut or a flutter beyond my consciousness.

My name is Amanda, I thought in my mind. *I'm here for you if you want to and are able to reach out.* I slowly let out the breath I'd been holding. *I'll wait right here by your side if you decide to make yourself known to me.*

And I waited. And waited. After twenty minutes, I knew it was time for me to leave. I slowly opened my eyes and looked at the woman who appeared to be sleeping peacefully. I wondered if her mind was at peace the way her body seemed to be. I was about to get up when I thought I heard a whisper. It was a tiny little sound that I wasn't even sure was real. I looked around the room, but there was no one there.

"Was that you?" I whispered back.

The heart monitor slowed. The light began to flash. Just before the alarm went off, I heard the word *aspen.*

"She's crashing," the nurse said. "I'll need you to leave."

I got up and walked out the door.

"What happened?" Trevor asked.

"I was trying to connect with Trinity and having no luck. I was about to leave when I heard a whisper. At first, I couldn't hear the voice clearly, but then the beeping on the heart rate monitor slowed. In the second after the alarm sounded, I heard her say *aspen.*"

"Is she... is she dead?"

I glanced back toward the room where the medical staff was working on her. "I don't know. I think she might have been for a minute. I think that is why I could hear her. The team came in with a crash cart immediately after I heard the whisper in my mind. I guess we'll just need to wait and see what happens."

Thirty minutes later, the nurse came out to tell us that Trinity was stable and resting comfortably. I thanked the nurse for letting me know and then Trevor and I left.

"You don't think she did that on purpose, do you?" Trevor asked.

"If you're asking if Trinity intentionally died so I could hear what she was trying to tell me, I don't see how she could have. I don't think someone can just will themselves dead. Can they?"

"I don't know, but the timing of everything is interesting. What if she could hear you trying to reach out to her, but she knew you couldn't hear what she was trying to tell you? What if when she realized you were going to leave, she decided to go all in? Maybe she knew the medical team would resuscitate her once she had delivered her message."

"Seems sort of unlikely, but maybe. Lord knows after everything I've seen, there isn't a lot I consider to be impossible."

"So, what now?" Trevor asked. "Do you still want to go by the courthouse and then have lunch, or do you want to go straight to Woody?"

"Woody. I have no idea what Trinity was trying to tell me, but maybe Woody will know what aspen means."

"It could be a name, and of course, it is a tree."

"Or it could be a place. There is an Aspen Drive in Cutter's Cove."

"And a park two towns over named Aspen Hollow," Trevor added. "Oh, and there is a housing development south of Cutter's Cove named Aspenwald. And there are a lot of aspen trees in the area, although I doubt she was referring to a tree."

"I guess we'll start by talking to Woody," I suggested. "He can talk to her boss and her sister and probably even get a look at her case files. If this woman actually died to provide me with this clue, you can darn well bet I'm going to figure out what it means."

I called Woody from the parking lot. He confirmed that he was in his office catching up on some paperwork, and I was welcome to come by. One of the men who worked under him was holding down the fort today in an official capacity, but Woody was the sort who could often be found in his office even on his day off.

"So what'd you find out?" He asked after Trevor and I sat down across from him.

I explained what happened at the hospital, including the revelation of the word aspen.

"The word aspen doesn't mean anything to me offhand, but you are correct in that it might be a name or a place. I'll call and speak to her boss and see if I can find out if she was working with any clients named Aspen or if any of her clients lived on Aspen Drive or in the Aspenwald housing development."

"You might call and speak to her sister," I suggested. "It occurred to us that Aspen could be a family member."

"I'll do that," Woody promised. "If I find anything relevant, I'll call you."

"So about the other shooting," Trevor jumped in. "Is there any truth to the rumor that Bryson Teller's wife is a suspect in his murder?"

Woody did this thing with his head that was sort of a nod and a shake. Based on the action, I couldn't tell if he was trying to offer an affirmative or negative response. Eventually, he answered. "These cases have hit close to home since Trinity and Bryson worked closely with law enforcement. Bryson particularly had friends in the DA's office, so of course, the rumors started off hot and furious from the moment he was shot. Bryson and his wife were indeed having marital issues, and their conflict had grown ugly as of late. I can see why there might be those who suspect her. Personally, I don't think she is the shooter we are looking for, nor do I believe she hired someone to shoot her husband. I think that there are some people who need immediate answers and that they've jumped on the first bandwagon they stumbled across, but I'm not giving a lot of credence to the rumors at this point."

"Do you have any actual suspects?" I asked.

"Detective Cobalter from the regional office has been assigned to take the lead on the case, although I am being kept up to date. As of this point, I know that no arrests have been made and that they are looking at Bryson's open and recently closed cases, as well as his personal life."

"So now that you've had the chance to collect additional data, are you thinking that Bryson and Trinity were shot by the same person?" I asked.

He frowned. "Honestly, I'm not sure. Logic would dictate that the shootings of two people in similar lines of work in a small town such as Cutter's

Cove within a twenty-four hour period would most likely be related, but short of proof one way or the other, I think the best thing I can do at this point is to look at the two cases as individual events. If a link between the two pops up, of course, I will pursue it."

"What about the open cases you mentioned earlier?" I asked.

Woody picked up a file. "As you remember, Trinity and Bryson were working on a child custody case involving the maternal grandfather of seven-year-old twins and their stepdad. The biological mother of the girls, a woman named Maria Brown, named her husband, Alton Brown, as guardian of her daughters, Connie and Aurora. Both Maria and Alton have a record, which made Maria's father, a man named Ben Bellingham, unhappy with his daughter's decision to name Alton as the one to raise her daughters in the event of her death. Immediately after Maria's death, Ben petitioned the court for custody of his granddaughters. Based on the notes I've read, it looked as if the grandfather was on the verge of getting what he was after, but then the biological father showed up and muddied things up by throwing his support behind the stepdad."

"I thought when we spoke earlier, you said the biological father was not involved in the lives of his daughters," I said.

"That was my understanding. If I had to guess, the stepdad and biological dad teamed up to defeat the grandfather. I'm not sure why, but both men are similar in that they seem to skirt the line between living productive lives and being in trouble with the law. Based on what I've found, it looks as if it was Maria's father who was behind Maria's decision to break up with Doug Cranmore, the biological father of the twins, and raise her babies on her own. When the girls were born, she was living with her father. I'm not sure at this point why Doug didn't ask for any sort of visitation with his children, but he didn't seem to pay child support, so I imagine the pair worked something out."

"So the biological father had reason to hold a grudge against the grandfather," Trevor said.

"Exactly," Woody answered. "I'm honestly not sure why the stepdad is so determined to raise the girls. On the surface, he seems to approach life much like an overgrown child, but in terms of his stepdaughters, he has fought the grandfather every step of the way."

"The situation does seem to be volatile, but I'm not sure why anyone involved would shoot either the social worker assigned to the case or the attorney arbitrating it," I said.

"All I know for certain at this point is that it appeared that both Trinity and Bryson were siding with the stepdad in spite of his spotty history."

"So the shooter might have been the grandfather," I said.

"Theoretically. I spoke to the man, and all I can say is that he is desperate to gain custody of his granddaughters. I also spoke to the stepdad, and while he does seem to be somewhat immature, the twins seem to adore him, and they look happy and well cared for. I'm not saying that the grandfather was the shooter. In fact, I would be surprised if he was, but the amount of rage he seems to be running on was somewhat frightening."

"If the grandfather was the shooter, wouldn't it make more sense to simply kill the stepdad if he wanted to get to the twins?" Trevor asked. "Why shoot the social worker and a family law attorney?"

"You make a good point, a point I made when speaking to the detective in charge of Bryson Teller's murder investigation. At this point, I have all the involved parties on my suspect list, but I don't have a strong feeling it will turn out to be any of them." Woody thumbed through the file. "However..."

"However?" I asked.

"The biological father does live in the Aspenwald subdivision. Still, if the biological father of Maria's girls was the one who shot Trinity, it seems that Trinity would have whispered Doug and not Aspen."

"I agree," I said. "I think the fact that this man lives in this specific subdivision is a coincidence. What else do you have? What about the neglect case involving the four children under ten?"

"As I stated before, initially Trinity was working with the parents, both who hold down two jobs, to rectify the fact that the children were left alone much of the time. After the oldest child set fire to the kitchen while trying to cook dinner for his younger siblings, Trinity decided that she had given the parents adequate time to fix the situation and that the best option at that point was to remove the children from their home. If you remember, the father of the children picked them up from school without permission with the intent of taking them to stay with his brother who lives out of state and in the end, he was arrested. While it does seem as if the father of these children might make a good suspect, he was still in custody when both Trinity and Bryson were shot."

"What about the mother?"

"She was at work when Bryson was shot. She doesn't have an alibi for the time that Trinity was shot, but while she struck me as being overworked and overwhelmed, she didn't strike me as being the sort to kill a person, or in this case, attempt to kill a person."

"And the children?" I asked. "Where are they now?"

"Foster homes."

"Are they together?" I wondered.

Woody picked up the file and read over the notes. "No. The four-year-old and the six-year-old are with a local family, the eight-year-old was placed with a family in the next town over, and the ten-year-old is currently in a group home."

"Do you think the parents were intentionally neglectful?" Trevor asked.

Woody looked up from the file. "Honestly, I don't think so. I think they made some bad choices. I think they could have done more to utilize the help Trinity tried to offer them, and I think that choosing to leave the children alone in the house was a very bad idea, but I also believe both parents love their children, and while the choices they made were poor, I don't think it was their intent to cause them harm."

"Anyone in the file named Aspen?" I asked.

Woody looked back at the file in his hands. His eyes grew large. "Actually, yes. The eight-year-old girl living in the foster home in the next town over is named Aspen Jenkins."

I glanced at Trevor. "Perhaps we should check on her."

Woody nodded. "Perhaps. I'll see what I can find out."

"And the third case we previously discussed? The one involving the fifteen-year-old whose mother was recently released from prison and has petitioned to have her son returned to her."

"At this point, it looks as if the case is in review, but there isn't any indication that the boy will be returned to the mother. The foster parents have planned all along to keep the child with them until he reaches maturity and would have adopted him long ago, but the mother refused to give up custody. It appears as if Trinity was siding with the foster parents, but I don't see any reason for anyone involved to have shot two people."

"Any reference to the word or name aspen in this case?" I asked.

Woody picked up the file and thumbed through. "Nope. Not a one." Woody set the file aside. "Now that I know we are looking for a person or place that links back to the clue Aspen, I'll do some more digging. I'll call and speak to both Trinity's sister and Bryson's boss. If I stumble across a smoking gun, I'll let you know."

"Okay," I said, standing up. "Trevor and I are going to go back to the courthouse and try one more time to connect with Bryson. My gut tells me he has moved on, but I do want to be sure. After that, we are going to go for a drive, but we'll be in cell range so call or text if anything comes up." I turned to leave. "Oh, and before I forget, Mom is making a big Thanksgiving dinner, and you are invited if you don't have other plans."

He looked pleased. "I'd like that very much."

"Great. I'll get back to you with a time, but Mom likes to eat a big holiday meal around mid-afternoon."

"Can I bring anything?" Woody asked.

"Probably not, but I'll check with Mom. I'm sure we'll talk multiple times between now and then." I took several steps toward the door. "And do let me know what you find out about eight-year-old Aspen. If she is in a bad situation or some sort of danger, I can see why Trinity might be willing to die to tell me."

"I'll check on her right now and call you when I know more."

Chapter 5

Trevor and I headed toward the courthouse after leaving Woody's office. I really wasn't expecting to find anything or anyone, but I figured I had to try. Since it was Saturday, the building was closed, which gave us the opportunity to look around the perimeter.

"Bryson was standing in the center of the taped off area when he was shot," I said to Trevor. "Court had just let out, and he was exiting the building. There were a lot of other people in the area, so the shooter must have been skilled to have picked him out the way he did." I turned in a full circle and tried to view the environment as the shooter would have. "Whoever shot Bryson must have already been in place and waiting for him." I turned and looked toward the office building across the street. "The shooter must have been set up over there."

"I agree with your assessment, but court let out a good two hours early on the day Bryson was shot. Do you think the shooter was just hanging around waiting?"

I shrugged. "It is the only thing that makes sense. Unless, of course, the shooter knew that court was going to be dismissed two hours early that day. I wonder what case was being heard."

"I guess Woody might know."

I nodded. "I guess he might."

"As far as where the shot was fired from, I heard that a shell casing was found on the roof of that building and that it is assumed that is where the shot was fired from," Trevor provided.

I shook my head. "I don't know. That doesn't feel right to me." Turning slightly, I tried to imagine Bryson walking out the door and down the stairs. I tried to imagine the path of the bullet as it traveled from the building across to street toward Bryson's chest. "If I had to guess, the shot was fired from one of the offices on the third or fourth floor and not from the roof."

"Why do you say that?"

"Just a hunch. The roof is too open. It seems that if the shot had come from there, someone would have seen something. But if the shot came from one of the offices within the building, the shooter could have easily slipped out unseen during the confusion."

"I guess it could have happened that way," Trevor admitted.

"We need to figure out which office."

"Since it is Saturday, most are closed today. I suppose we can call Woody and he can try to get a warrant to search the building. Actually, given the situation, he might not even need a warrant. I think most of those offices are publically owned offices."

I shook my head. "That will take too long. I have a better idea. Alyson," I called.

She appeared. "What's up?"

"See the office building across the street?"

"Yeah."

"I need you to pop into all the offices on the third and fourth floor. Take a look around and then come back and let me know if you find anything odd."

"Odd how?"

"I think a sniper set up in one of those offices. Just look for an office that appears to be vacant or an office where the furniture looks to have been moved around recently. That sort of thing."

"Okay. I'm on it." She disappeared.

I turned to Trevor. "Alyson is taking a look around. I'm going to see if I can connect to Bryson's spirit while we're waiting."

"Do you think he is here?" Trevor asked while I searched for the best place to sit and meditate.

"Honestly, no, but I do want to be sure."

Heading across the courtyard to a bench beneath a dormant tree, I sat down and closed my eyes. Relaxing my mind, I focused on Bryson, inviting him in should he be in the area. As I suspected, I connected with no one. Eventually, I opened my eyes and looked at Trevor. "He's not here. I really think he moved on immediately after his death."

"I guess that's a good thing. For him, at least."

"It is."

Alyson appeared next to me. "So?"

"So what?" Trevor asked.

"Sorry. I was talking to Alyson. She's back." I turned my attention back toward Alyson. "So?"

"The third office over from the end on the left side of the building on the fourth floor is empty and unoccupied and based on the amount of dust, I am going to say it has been unoccupied for quite some time. The second office over from the end on the same side on the third floor is likewise unoccupied, but it looks like the space might have had tenants a bit more recently. There are still a few random pieces of furniture inside each of the offices."

"Okay, good. Did you notice anything in either office that stood out as having been the office used for the shooting?"

"Like what?"

"A sniper rifle, for example."

"No. There was nothing like that. Although the office on the fourth floor did show scuff marks in the dust on the floor as if something had been moved recently."

"Okay, thanks. Before you go, can you sense the man who was shot? Is his spirit still around?"

Alyson shook her head. "No. I think he must have already moved on."

"That's what I thought as well. You can go, but stay close. I may need you again."

Alyson glanced at Trevor and then back at me. "So how hot was that makeout session last night?"

I was sure I blushed. I wanted to tell Alyson to mind her own business, although I supposed her business and mine were the same business, but Trevor was standing right next to me, so I simply sent her a dirty look as she disappeared.

"Did she find anything?" Trevor asked.

I filled him in. "I'm going to call Woody and suggest he come by and take a closer look at both offices and then you and I can go to lunch."

"Sounds good. I'm starving."

Woody promised to head over to the office building and have another look around. He did bring up the fact that a shell casing had been found on the roof, to which I responded that the casing could have been left there as a decoy. It would have been pretty sloppy of the shooter to leave a casing behind that might be traced back to him, and the man who shot Bryson had done so with such accuracy that it appeared he was a professional sniper. Woody agreed with my assessment after we chatted a while and assured me that he would look into things.

Once that was accomplished, Trevor and I piled into his truck for lunch and a drive down the coast. As crazy as our idea might be to investigate the shootings and to enjoy what was left of our impromptu vacation, that was exactly what I intended to do.

"It looks like there might be a storm gathering on the horizon," Trevor glanced out toward the sea.

Dark clouds were gathering in the distance in spite of the beautiful morning we'd started the day with. "I wonder if we are going to get rain. I didn't notice rain in the forecast, but I wouldn't be surprised to get some. It seems as if has been a relatively dry fall."

"I guess we might end up with some rain, but it is just as likely the clouds will hang around offshore and never come any closer than they are. Do you still want seafood for lunch?"

"Anything is fine. I know our original plan has been altered somewhat."

"Since we are heading south, there is that cute little place on the water where I took you when we went antiquing that day."

I nodded. "That sounds perfect. I've been meaning to get back there, but so far, it hasn't worked out. We could even stop by the Antique Barn. I wouldn't mind looking around a bit. I still want to find a pair of bedside tables to go with the dresser I bought the last time we were there."

"I wouldn't mind stopping." Trevor placed his hand over mine.

I wondered if we should talk about what happened last night or if it would be better to pretend that the electricity between us wasn't powerful enough to blow a circuit. Opting for easy and casual, I made a comment about the fall colors and the late start to the change of seasons this year.

Lunch was delicious. I opted for a seafood salad, and Trevor went for clam chowder in a bread bowl. We shared a piece of cheesecake while we discussed the upcoming holiday season and our plans for the next six weeks or so. It felt good to be making plans to do fun and silly things like visiting Santa's Village and eating corndogs at the Christmas Carnival. When I'd lived in New York, I'd enjoyed the decorations, and I always stopped to watch the ice skaters at Rockefeller Center, but I'm pretty sure I never ate a single corndog or rode a single carousel the entire time I lived there. I was looking forward to enjoying the sort of fun I engaged in during the long-ago Christmases Trevor, Mac, and I had spent together.

"So should we head to the Antique Barn?" Trevor asked after we'd paid the bill and returned to his truck.

"Hang on. I have a missed call from Woody."

"Did he leave a message?"

I switched over to my voicemail. "He did." I listened to it.

"What's up? You're frowning," Trevor said.

"It's Aspen. The eight-year-old who is in foster care as a result of being taken from her parents. She ran away. I guess she was last seen by her foster parents on Thursday evening. I'm going to call Woody and see if he has additional information."

According to Woody, the last time Aspen was seen was Thursday evening when she went up to her room after dinner. She'd been angry and prickly since she'd been at the foster home, so her foster parents decided to give her some space. When her foster mother went up to her room on Friday morning to wake her, she wasn't there. They hadn't heard her leave, but they did find that some of Aspen's clothing as well as the money from her foster mother's purse were missing. The police in the town where the foster family lives have been looking for her ever since. When Woody called to check in on her, he was given an update. Apparently, there was a call from the house phone where Aspen had been living to Trinity's cell on the day Trinity was shot. No one knows what the two talked about, but less than three hours later, Trinity was in a coma and Aspen had been seen for the last time.

"Wow, I hope she is okay," Trevor said.

"Yeah. Me too."

"What have they done to find her?"

"They've interviewed her mother as well as her older brother, who is living in the group home. Both of whom say they have not heard from her. The father is still being detained for taking his children from school without permission. The police officer who responded to the call from the foster parents has apparently been talking to other family members, including the uncle her father was trying to drop his children off with. At this point, no one knows where she is." I answered.

"Is there anything we can do?" Trevor asked.

Pursing my lips, I slowly shook my head. "I don't know. I feel like Trinity gave me her name for a reason. We know that Trinity and Aspen spoke on the day Trinity was shot. I suppose it is possible that Trinity had made plans to meet up with Aspen or maybe Aspen had called to let her know that she was taking off unless she was returned to her parents, or perhaps the foster parents were cruel to her and Aspen was calling her social worker to complain. It seems obvious to me that Trinity is concerned about the girl. We really do need to find her. I'm just not sure how to go about doing so."

"Maybe her older brother has an idea where she might go. If the police officer in charge of looking for Aspen has spoken to him and he denied knowing anything, and it was the police who helped to break up his family, chances are he doesn't trust them. Maybe Woody can arrange for us to talk to the child. It might not do any good, but I wouldn't think it could hurt," Trevor suggested.

"It's worth a try. I'll call Woody and see if he can set it up."

******

The group home Billy was living in seemed nice in an institutional sort of way. The house was large and laid out to provide most of the kids with at least a small amount of personal space, and the yard was large enough to play in. The bedrooms were small, but the common area with a television and game table was fairly large, as were the kitchen and dining area. The only full-time residents were the kids who lived there, as the staff came in shifts that rotated each day.

We elected to meet with Billy outside even though there was a chill to the air. Since it was Saturday, the kids were home from school, and the interior of the house was crowded and loud. We settled in at a picnic table on the back deck and introduced ourselves. I could see that all of Billy's shields were up from the moment he was sent out to speak to us.

"I guess someone has already been by to speak to you about Aspen," I started off. "And I know you told the officer you didn't know where she was or where she might be headed. And I realize you don't know us so have no reason to believe anything we say, but I promise you we only want to help. We are afraid that Aspen could be in danger and we want to help find her before she is hurt. We need you to help us with that."

The boy narrowed his eyes but didn't speak.

"I'm sure you are worried about Aspen as well," Trevor jumped in. "And I bet you wish you had someone you could trust to help find her. Am I right?"

The boy didn't look up or respond.

"I know you are angry with the police for taking you away from your family and detaining your father when he was just trying to help you find a better solution than foster care. And I don't blame you a bit. But this isn't about helping the police, this is about helping Aspen," I added.

"How can you help?" he asked, rage evident in his voice.

"Amanda here is a superhero," Trevor said.

The boy glanced at me. I could see that he was interested.

"She knows things and can even read minds," he elaborated.

"Prove it."

Trevor looked at me. I nodded. "We'll send Amanda away, so she doesn't hear our plan, and then we'll call her back."

"Okay."

Standing, I walked across the yard. Once I was out of earshot, I called to Alyson. She must have been lurking and knew what was going on since once she appeared, she simply said, "I'm on it" and then disappeared. After a moment, Trevor called me back.

Alyson appeared. "Billy has a frog named Homer. One of the other kids let him go, and Billy is really upset. There is a large frog under the rock near the oak tree. I'm not sure that frog is Billy's frog, but it seems likely."

"Okay. Thanks." I headed back to Billy and Trevor.

"Billy has a pet we discussed while you were across the yard. He wants to know if you know what sort of pet he is and what his name is." Trevor asked.

"Billy's pet is a frog named Homer," I answered. "He is lost, and I think..." I walked over to the tree and lifted the rock, praying the whole time that the frog would be there and that it would be the right frog, "this is where he has been hiding."

Billy smiled. "Homer." He ran over and picked up the frog.

Thank you, I sent a mental thanks to Alyson, God, the universe, and any and all otherworld powers that may have actually led me to the one thing that would get Billy to trust me.

Billy looked at me. "You really are a superhero. Can you find Aspen?"

"I don't know, but I'd like to try. With your help, of course. Do you have any idea where she might have gone or where she might be headed?"

"I don't know for sure where Aspen went, but we do have a place we'd go when we needed to hide."

"Hide? Hide from who?"

"Just people. I don't want to talk about it, and it doesn't matter. Before I show you where the secret spot is, I need to know what you are going to do with Aspen. I'm not going to tell you where she might be just so you can send her back to the same place she went to so much trouble to escape from."

I glanced at Trevor. He shrugged. I supposed once we tracked Aspen down, sending her back was exactly what would happen. "Is there someone you and Aspen could stay with? Someone who the people from child services might trust to watch out for you."

"My uncle."

"The uncle who lives in Utah?"

Billy nodded.

"That might be a long term solution, but I don't think it will work out in the short term. Do you have any relatives living here in the area?" I asked.

Billy slowly shook his head.

"Okay. Let me make a couple of phone calls."

It took some doing, but eventually, I was able to convince Woody to pull some strings so that both Billy and Aspen could stay with me at least until a permanent solution could be found for all four children. He needed time to call in some favors and make this happen, so in the short term, I got him to agree to allow Billy, Trevor, and me to look for Aspen free and clear of any promise or expectation that we would turn her over to him or anyone in child services once we found her. He mumbled something about losing his job, but eventually, he agreed that he would not ask about our success in finding the girl, thereby putting us all in a difficult situation until he had worked out the details.

Once I'd spoken to Woody, I explained the plan to Billy. I don't think he believed we could help, but after Woody managed to get the group home to turn Billy over to us for a twenty-four-hour visit, I think he started to believe we were actually on his side.

After having worked with both law enforcement and child services, I knew that the men and women who'd committed their lives to protect the children really did have their best interest at heart. Yes, at times the red tape mucked things up, but generally speaking, if a good alternative was offered, the folks who oversaw such things did what they could to make whatever was in the best interest of the child work out.

Billy led us to a trail near the home he'd shared with his family. He told us to park on the street, and then he led us through the woods to the beach. We walked down the beach a bit until we came to a small opening in the bluff. "Wait here," he said. "If Aspen is here, she will be scared if she sees you."

Trevor and I agreed to wait while Billy disappeared inside the crevice, which I assumed connected to the cave system that existed in the area.

"Do you really think an eight-year-old could make it all the way over here from the foster home where she was staying?" Trevor asked.

"She did have money, and from what I've heard, these kids are pretty street smart, having been on their own so much."

"I guess."

I looked around the area to see if anyone was nearby, but the place looked to be deserted. "I just hope we can figure out a way to get all four of them back together. I haven't made up my mind about the parents yet. Based on what Woody said, it sounds as if Trinity really tried to help the parents do what they needed to do to keep their children, but they chose to ignore her counsel. Maybe the kids would be better off with the uncle or maybe with someone else."

"I guess that is up to the courts to figure out."

Billy squeezed back through the crack. A young girl who I assumed was Aspen followed behind him.

"I'm so glad you are okay," I smiled gently at the girl whose pigtails hung to the side as she stared intently at the ground. Her clothes were filthy, and her eyes looked much too large in her thin face. My heart really went out to her.

"Are you going to take me back?" she asked in a quiet voice.

"No, I'm not going to take you back. I'm not sure what is going to happen in the long run, but right now Trevor and I are going to take both of you to my house. I arranged for you to stay with me until we can figure this out."

Aspen looked terrified. Billy took her hand in his. "It's okay. Amanda is a superhero. She'll help us stay together."

Lord did I hope that was true.

Chapter 6

Of course, once my mom realized there were children in the house, she took them under her wing and started clucking after them like the protective mama hen she was. Both Billy and Aspen were thrilled to see that the house not only had two dogs but a cat as well. I knew their stay with us would be temporary, but I wanted to be sure that they'd be comfortable while they were here. We gave them something to eat, and then I texted Woody to let him know that the children were with us and had settled in for the time being. He texted back and said that he had gotten permission for both Billy and Aspen to stay with us until Monday when the new social worker could officially look into things.

Placing foster kids with people who were not related to the child, and had not been certified by child services was not the norm, but Woody managed to convince social services that returning them to the homes they'd been in would most likely result in one or both running away, so it was agreed they could stay with us until something else was worked out.

Once I'd settled Billy and Aspen with my mom, I decided to go back to the hospital to assure Trinity that we'd found Aspen and that she was being taken care of. I wasn't sure she'd hear me, but in the event she could, I really wanted her to know that her sacrifice in momentarily dying had done what she hoped the clue she provided to me would do.

Woody had called ahead to clear the way for me to visit, but this time when I arrived with Trevor on my heels, Trinity's sister, Carmen, was there.

"How is she doing?" I asked Carmen.

"The same. She seems to be resting comfortably, but she still hasn't regained consciousness. After the scare this morning, I'm just happy she is still alive. The nurse said you were sitting with her when she crashed. Do you have any idea what happened?"

"Not specifically. I was sitting with her, trying to get a reading in the event she knows who shot her. When she crashed, I picked up the word aspen. I did some research and found out that one of the kids in her caseload is named Aspen. She'd recently been put into the foster care system and had run away. Aspen had called Trinity shortly before she was shot. I suspect your sister knew she was in trouble and tried to reach out to me. I'm actually here now to let your sister know I heard her and that I was able to help Aspen. In fact, she is staying with me at my home until we can work things out next week."

"Do you think that trying to reach out to you is what caused her heart to stop?"

"I'm not sure," I answered honestly.

"Perhaps it would be best if you didn't sit with her any longer. I wouldn't be able to bear it if I lost her."

"I understand your concern, and of course, I will honor your wish. I would like to tell her I found Aspen and that she is safe. I don't know if she can hear me, but in the event she can, I think she will want to know."

"Okay. I guess that will be fine."

I left the hospital not knowing whether or not Trinity had heard me, but I did feel good about the fact that between the two of us we'd found Aspen and made sure she was safe and that her needs were being heard and considered. Part of me really wanted to try to connect again in the event Trinity had more to tell me, but I understood where Carmen was coming from. If it was my sister's life on the line, I wouldn't want to do anything to put it at risk either.

"So where to now?" Trevor asked once we'd left the hospital.

"I guess let's stop off at the store and pick up some kid food and then go back to the house and help mom out." I slid into the passenger seat of the truck. "I'm sorry. This isn't working out to be the staycation we hoped for after our actual vacation fell apart."

"It's not a problem at all. Anything we can do to make things easier for those kids is worth doing. Maybe I'll stop by my place and pick up my video game system. Billy is the right age to enjoy blowing stuff up."

"I think that is a wonderful idea."

Trevor walked around the truck and slid into the driver's seat. He turned and looked at me. "Do you think Billy and Aspen need clothing and toothbrushes and whatnot?"

"I'm sure we can stop by the group home and pick up what we need for Billy, but Aspen might need stuff."

"She was wearing that backpack when we found her."

"I'll call my mom and see what she has with her and what she might need."

Mom gave me a small list of items to pick up and assured me that she had things handled for the time being. Both kids had been through a lot in the past few weeks, and both seemed happy to curl up in the den with the animals and watch cartoons. It had begun to sprinkle, and the dark clouds that had been on the horizon earlier had begun to move inland. I had a feeling we were going to be in for a good amount of rain before this was all over.

"As long as we are stopping at your place to get the video game system, why don't you grab Pj's and a toothbrush. If the storm gets too bad, you can stay at my place tonight."

Trevor playfully wiggled his eyebrows. "Sounds like your idea has promise."

"You can sleep in the third-floor guest room," I clarified. "I'm sure it won't be as comfy as your own bed, but if it really starts coming down hard, you will have the option to stay if you want."

"Thanks for the offer. I might take you up on your suggestion, so I'll grab a few things. I'm not afraid of a little rain, but with the way this vacation has been going so far, I suppose I should be prepared for anything."

"I wonder if Mac and Ty are having better luck with their attempt for some couple time. I'm not even sure where they went. All she said was that they were going down the coast."

"I had the feeling that Mac was being intentionally vague," Trevor said. "I don't think she wants to be found."

"I guess I don't blame her. It does seem like she and Ty have had been trying to get some alone time for a while now and they keep getting interrupted."

Trevor pulled into his drive and parked. We both got out and went inside. He headed toward the entertainment center and began to unplug his video game system. I walked across the room and looked out at the sea, which was pounding onto the beach. The thought of cuddling up with Trevor and watching it rain was so tempting, but it appeared as if we'd have Billy and Aspen to look after at least for the next few days. Given the fact that next week was Thanksgiving, it wouldn't surprise me if we had them all week. I wondered if the courts were even in session next week. Perhaps for a day or two at the beginning of the week; hopefully, long enough to make a more permanent arrangement for the siblings.

I really felt bad for those kids. Given the fact that it appeared they'd needed to be fairly self-sufficient, I would be willing to bet the four siblings were really close. I wondered about the younger two. I hoped there was a way to reunite the family. Somehow, the idea of them all going in separate directions just didn't seem right.

"Ready?" Trevor asked after a few minutes.

"I am. Did you get what you needed?"

"I did. Was there anything else you wanted to do before heading back to your place other than stopping by the group home to get Billy's things and the store to pick up supplies?"

"No. I guess not. I keep feeling like I should be doing more to help Woody find the person who shot Trinity and Bryson, but Bryson has moved on, and Trinity isn't dead, so I guess my unique skill set isn't really a factor at this point in time."

"In this instance, I think you are right that there really isn't anything we can do to help. If things change and it looks like there is something we can do, we'll figure it out from there."

Standing on tiptoe. I kissed Trevor on the mouth. "Thank you."

He tightened his arms around me and kissed me back. "I'm not sure what I've done to deserve such a sweet thank you, but if this is the reward, whatever it was, was totally worth it."

I ran a finger across Trevor's cheek while looking into his eyes. "Thank you for being you. Thank you for caring. Thank you for giving up your vacation to help these kids. I know this is not the intimate getaway you hoped for. We both hoped for," I clarified.

Trevor leaned in slightly and captured my lips for just a moment. "I think we are doing exactly what we need to do, and if all we accomplish today is helping Billy and Aspen through this difficult time, then I think that is enough."

When we arrived at the house, we found Billy and Aspen curled up together on the sofa like puppies. Both were sound asleep.

"I could see the kids were exhausted, so I went ahead and gave them dinner," Mom informed me. "If you and Trevor want to carry them upstairs and get their pajamas on, I'll start dinner for the three of us."

"I'm sorry your dinner plans were ruined," I said, remembering for the first time that Mom had had plans this evening.

"It's not a problem at all. Making sure the kids are okay is much more important."

"They certainly have had a tough time of it," Trevor agreed.

"They are both really worried about their younger siblings," Mom said. "I'm sure they are fine, but I can also see why the older two are worried. They are used to taking care of the little ones. I'm wondering if Woody can arrange a visit. I'd be happy to supervise if the younger two would be allowed to come over for a while tomorrow."

"I'll call Woody in the morning and see if there is anything we can work out." I glanced at Trevor, who was leaning over to pick up Billy. "In the meantime, we'll get them settled in bed. I'm going to put them both in the guestroom with the king-sized bed on the second floor."

"That's a great idea. I think they'll find comfort in each other's company," Mom agreed.

After we carried the children upstairs, Trevor helped Billy into his pajamas, and I helped Aspen into hers. An odd thought of us doing this in the future for our own children flashed into my mind. I don't know if the thought was a potent or simply a daydream, but I had to admit it left me with a warm and fuzzy feeling and not the terror the idea of children had caused in the past.

Once we'd tucked them in, we went downstairs to join Mom in the kitchen.

"I'm just making an omelet for the three of us since we had the ingredients and it sounded easy," Mom informed us.

"Sounds good to me."

"I have biscuits in the oven. It's been a while since I've made biscuits. Seemed like just the thing on a rainy night."

I glanced out the window. The rain was coming down steady now, and the wind had picked up quite a bit.

"Any news from Woody on either shooting?" Mom asked as she poured the beaten eggs into a pan.

"No. I thought I'd call him tomorrow. I don't want to take up a lot of his time since I know he has his hands full, but I will admit to being curious as to whether he thinks the two events are related."

"It seems that two shootings involving individuals who both work in the area of family law would be related," Mom pointed out.

"You would think so, but while both were shot, each was shot with a different type of gun. I'm just not sure that a shooting at close range with a handgun and a shooting from a distance with a sniper rifle would be carried out by the same person."

"Maybe the fact that two different weapons were used was intended to throw everyone off," Trevor offered.

"Perhaps," I agreed. "And I do agree that the fact that Trinity and Bryson worked together on the same cases would seem to indicate that an unhappy client was behind things. I'm not unhappy that Trinity directed me toward Aspen. If I'd had time to provide only a single clue, that is what I'd have done as well, but I do wish we'd had time for her to tell me who shot her. I just have this feeling she knows."

"Maybe she'll wake up," Mom said.

"I hope so. And not just because she can probably direct us to the person who shot her. I'd never even heard her name before this, but I can tell that she is a very special woman."

"Do you know if she's married? Does she have children of her own?" Mom asked.

Hesitating, I answered. "I'm not really certain, but it has been her sister who has been staying by her side at the hospital. No one has mentioned a husband or children. At least not to me. She's young. Mid- to late-twenties. I imagine she might have been focusing on her career to this point."

Mom scooped the omelet onto a plate and divided it into thirds. She took the biscuits from the oven and slid them into a basket. I grabbed the coffee pot, and we all headed to the little table in the kitchen nook. The table was small and only accommodated four chairs, three comfortably, but the nook was really more of a large garden window, which allowed us to enjoy the storm while staying dry.

"So about Thanksgiving," Mom said, totally changing the subject. "My friend is not going to be able to come due to a family emergency back in Nebraska, but I was chatting with Donovan and almost jokingly suggested he should hop over and join us, and he agreed."

"Wow." I raised a brow. "That's great. I am surprised he is willing to fly clear across the country for dinner, but I'm thrilled. I haven't seen him in forever."

"I couldn't have been more surprised when he accepted my invitation," Mom agreed. "Not that it was even meant as a real invitation given the distance, but now that he has accepted, I agree with you, I really can't wait to see him."

"So do you chat with Donovan often?" Donovan had been my handler when I'd been in witness protection and Mom and I had occasionally checked in with him but until I'd received some odd texts a while back that we felt might be related to the mob family who'd wanted me dead in the first place, I hadn't talked to him in several years.

"I've been staying in contact with him ever since you received the texts and the photo of the Bonatello brothers. I know that Donovan isn't overly worried since it appears that the person who sent the texts believes you are in New York, but as your mother, I can't help but be worried. Talking things through with Donovan helps."

The text I'd received back in October contained a photo of Clay and Mario Bonatello, the brothers who killed my best friend and tried to kill me, landing me in witness protection, along with a message: *She who spills the blood must pay the price.* Donovan believed Vito Bonatello, Clay's son, might have sent the message. Their own family members had taken out both Clay and Mario after it was decided by the group that their obsession with me was bad for everyone involved. Vito had been in jail when his father had been murdered but had recently gotten out. Since he'd been out, five top-ranking members of the Bonatello family had been murdered, including Franco Bonatello, the highest-ranking family member and the one who had given the go-ahead to have Vito's father killed.

"Did Donovan have any news?" I asked.

"Not really. He has been keeping a close eye on things and was somewhat concerned about the break-in at your old apartment, but he also said that things have been quiet for a while."

Donovan had had one of the FBI guys from the Portland office pick up my phone. He was monitoring all my incoming texts and calls. In the meantime, I'd been given an unregistered burner cell to use.

"I'm happy that Donovan is coming for a visit. I miss him. But I'm not going to get pulled into worrying about something that I might not even need to worry about. I'm sorry this is upsetting for you, but I do hope you can relax and enjoy the holiday."

"I will. And I am. I do feel better being here where I can keep an eye on you."

I leaned over and gave Mom a hug. "I know. And I feel better about the fact that you are here watching over me as you always have."

Chapter 7

Sunday, November 18

I woke the following morning to the sound of laughter coming from downstairs. Children's laughter. It was nice. I smiled as I laid in bed and stared at the ceiling. Tucker was lying on the bed next to me, but Sunny and Shadow were both missing. I assumed Mom had opened my door and let them out when she and kids had gotten up. Trevor had ended up staying as well, so it seemed we had a full house this morning.

I turned my head and stared into the brown eyes of my best buddy. "Are you ready to get up?"

He thumped his tail on the bed.

"Sounds hectic." I laid there for another minute. "But nice."

I wasn't the sort who minded being alone, but it was nice when the house came alive with the sound of voices. Sliding my legs to the side, I pulled myself out of bed. Padding into the attached bath, I brushed my teeth, washed my face, and pulled on a pair of jeans and a sweatshirt. I really hadn't meant to sleep as late as I had, but I guess I'd been tired. Between the cruise gone wrong and the recent shootings, it had been a stressful week.

When I arrived downstairs, I found Aspen in the kitchen, mixing up something that looked like cookie dough and Billy in the den killing zombies with Trevor. Sunny growled at the zombies every time they exploded, while Shadow was curled up in a chair watching the show.

"There she is," Trevor greeted after hitting pause on the game.

"Sorry I slept so long. Did you both get breakfast?" I asked.

"Your mom made a breakfast casserole," Trevor answered. "She has some warming in the oven for you."

"Okay. I'm going to go and grab some coffee. I don't want to interrupt your game."

I wasn't even out the door before I heard the sound of Zombie explosions starting back up in the background.

"Are you hungry?" Mom asked.

"Actually I think, I'll just start with coffee for now. Are you making cookies?"

"Apricot oatmeal," Aspen answered.

"That sounds yummy."

"Woody called for you about an hour ago," my mom informed me. "I offered to wake you, but he said it could wait. He said to have you call him as soon as you got up."

I poured a cup of coffee and then took a sip. "Okay, thanks. I'll call him now."

Deciding to head back upstairs where it was quieter, I grabbed my coffee and my cell and headed in that direction.

"Hey, Woody. It's Amanda. What's up?" I asked after he picked up.

"I called to update you on the Bryson Teller shooting, and to ask a favor, but before I get into that, when I called this morning your mom answered your cell, and once she had me on the line she managed to manipulate me into agreeing to facilitate a visit between Billy and Aspen and their younger siblings."

I laughed. "I'm not surprised. Last night, she mentioned that Billy and Aspen were worried about them and she felt that a visit would help and if I know my mom, and I do, I also know that once she latches onto an idea, she won't be letting go anytime soon."

"I figured as much, so I made some calls. As it turns out, the woman who was assigned to oversee Trinity's cases, at least for the time being, is an old friend of mine and she agreed to try to arrange a visit. Leslie was able to reach the foster family who took the younger two siblings, and it seems they are really overcrowded and wondered if you would be willing to take the younger two in until a more permanent situation can be worked out."

Four kids? Four was a lot, but I knew Mom would be all over it. "I'll check with Mom, but I think that will be fine. I seem to remember the younger two are four and six."

"Willow is four, and Henry is six. If your mom is willing to take responsibility for them, I can have then brought to you today."

"I'll ask her and call you right back. You said you had a favor you wanted to ask?"

"Check with your mom first, and then when you call back, we can discuss the favor."

"Okay. I'll ask her right now. In fact, if you just want to hang on, that might be faster."

As I expected, Mom was more than willing to keep an eye on all four children if they could be together. I told Woody as much, and he promised to make the arrangements. I figured two could sleep in the bed on the third floor and two could sleep in the bed on the second floor. Since Mom's room and mine were on the second floor, I supposed it would be best to put the older two upstairs.

"Okay, now for the favor," Woody said. "I've managed to dig up a few suspects in the Bryson Teller shooting. None are great suspects, but they do have a motive. I know you've gone to the courthouse twice and have not been able to connect, but I remembered you told me once before that while most of the time a ghost will be found where they died, there are instances when they will return to a specific place like their home."

"That is true."

"I wondered if you would be willing to go by Bryson's home just to check to see if he is there. He recently separated from his wife and moved into a new house on the coast just south of Cutter's Cove. I have no idea if he would even think of it as home at this point, but I did want to eliminate the possibility that he might be hanging out there. If he hasn't moved on as we suspect he has, then maybe he knows something that will help us to pin down the person who killed him."

Glancing out the window, I sighed. At least the rain had stopped. "I'd be happy to go to his home and see if I can connect. How do I get in?"

"I'll meet you there. You need a code to get in the gate at the front of the neighborhood and then a key and alarm code to get into the house."

"Okay. Give me an hour. Oh, and I'll need an address."

******

As Woody had indicated, Bryson lived in a gated community just south of Cutter's Cove. The house, while beautiful, was sparse in terms of personal accents. There were no paintings on the walls, no photos on the mantel, and no magazines, takeout menus, or stacks of mail that would indicate that anyone actually lived there, but it did sound as if he'd only recently moved out of the home he'd shared with his wife. I really doubted that Bryson was here. As Woody had already suggested, the man hadn't really had time to form an emotional attachment to the place or to even make it into a place that felt like home. Still, I had come all this way, so I decided to try to connect as long as I was here. I didn't sense the man, so I decided to just walk around the house, touching things in the hope I'd get a feel for his spirit if he was indeed still with us.

Walking into the kitchen, I opened the refrigerator. Beer, water, and fruit in the main compartment, nothing in the freezer. I supposed the guy ate out most of the time. I didn't blame him. The house didn't have that warm and cozy feel that would make a person want to spend a lot of time there. The cupboards were likewise empty except for coffee pods, granola bars, and protein powder. There was a rack with wine bottles on the kitchen counter and a cupboard with a variety of glassware. A half-full bottle of scotch sat next to a used glass on the island. It looked as if Bryson had come home the night before he was shot, had a drink or two, then most likely retired to the master bedroom. I headed toward the hallway.

Most of the rooms had no furniture. The master bedroom was the only room that looked occupied. It featured an unmade king-sized bed, a tall armoire, a walk-in closet, a flat-screen TV, and several chairs, all with clothing draped over them. There was a table near the window which overlooked the water. A printer and cables for a laptop, which I assumed Bryson had with him when he was shot, sat on the table.

Woody, who was waiting outside with Trevor, had given me a photo of Bryson. I sat on the corner of the bed, closed my eyes, and tried to focus on his photo. Most of the time, when a ghost came to me, it simply appeared. Either Bryson really was gone, or he was playing hard to get.

"Bryson, if you can hear me, my name is Amanda. I can see ghosts if they want to be seen, so if you are here, it would be awesome if you would appear." I opened my eyes. Nothing. "I realize you don't know me and have no reason to trust me, but I work with the police and am trying to figure out who shot you. If you have any information at all that might help narrow down the suspect list, revealing what you know would be much appreciated."

Sitting quietly, I waited. I didn't see him, or anyone for that matter, but I did feel a presence. The presence was faint. So faint, in fact, that I wasn't sure that what I was feeling was even a presence. If Bryson wasn't here or wasn't willing to appear, then I didn't want to waste my time by sitting here all day, but if he was just shy, I didn't want to leave too soon.

I was about to give up and return to the guys when I heard a crash in the walk-in closet. I opened the door, turned on the light, and stepped inside. It looked as though a shoebox had fallen from the shelf onto the floor. "Bryson?"

Still, no one appeared. I picked up the shoebox and looked inside. Black dress shoes that appeared to be new were inside the shoebox. I was about to replace the shoebox, but I decided to take the shoes out to make sure there wasn't anything significant about them, like a hidden compartment in the heel. When I took the right shoe out of the box, a small gold key fell to the floor. I bent over and picked it up. "Okay," I said, turning the key over in my hand. "What do you open?"

I looked around the bedroom, but I didn't find a locked cabinet or drawer of any kind. I returned to the closet and began moving clothes to the side. Three drawers were on the wall behind the clothes. The top drawer held socks, the second drawer boxers, but the bottom drawer was locked. Using the key, I unlocked and then opened the drawer to find files. I lifted them out. I wasn't certain they were relevant to the shooting but decided to take them with me. It seemed odd to me that Bryson would have files in a locked drawer in the back of his closet. A file cabinet or a desk with locking drawers would have made a lot more sense.

"Anything?" Woody asked when I returned to the porch where the guys were hanging out.

Holding up the files, I shrugged. "Bryson didn't appear, but a shoebox containing a pair of shoes fell to the floor from a shelf. I found a key inside the right shoe that opened a locked drawer at the back of the closet. These files were in the drawer."

"And the other drawers?"

"Just socks and boxers," I said.

Woody took the files. "I suppose the files could contain a clue. Especially if it was Bryson who led you to the key. Let's go back to my office and see what sort of things Bryson was working on during his off-hours."

******

Once we arrived at Woody's office, he ushered us to the conference room. He set the files on the conference table while he made a pot of coffee. There were six files in the stack. As Woody had, I wondered if one of those six files might point us toward Bryson Teller's killer.

Once the coffee was made, Woody poured the dark liquid into three mugs and then joined Trevor and me at the table. He reached for the first file and opened it. After a moment, he began to speak.

"This file pertains to the case I mentioned before relating to the fifteen-year-old who has been in the foster care system since he was four. If you remember, both of his parents were sent to prison for armed robbery. As I've already mentioned, the boy's mother was recently released from prison early due to overcrowding and for good behavior. She has petitioned to have her son returned to her. When the foster parents accepted the child, they had been told that the boy's parents would be in prison until after he was eighteen, so having him returned to either parent wouldn't be an issue. They are fighting the mother's petition and are arguing that the boy will be better off with them."

"And the boy?" I asked.

"He has stated that he would like to stay where he is. He has very few memories of his biological mother and those memories he does have are tainted with fear. Based on these notes, it looks as if Bryson was representing the fifteen-year-old, and it looks, based on his notes, that he didn't anticipate there being a problem with arranging things so that the boy could stay in the foster home."

"Did you ever speak to the mother?" I asked, remembering that he had intended to.

"I have. The woman seems remorseful about the decisions she made in the past. She was a model prisoner during her incarceration, and her desire to be reunited with her son seems to be based on genuine caring. She'd been working with Trinity to try to find a way into her son's life. What the mother really wants is to have custody returned to her, but since the boy is doing so well with his foster family, and it was his desire to stay where he is, Trinity seemed to be leaning toward a recommendation that the mother be given supervised visits, but that the custody issue be left as is for the time being."

"It sounds like neither Trinity nor Bryson supported the mother's desire to regain custody of her son. Do you think the woman might have taken matters into her own hands to remove the opposition?"

"Actually, I don't. The biological mother made a lot of bad choices in the past, but she has done her time and is ready for a second chance. She seems to be doing everything required of her as part of her early release, and I don't think she'd muck that up by going on a shooting spree. While she was unable to provide an alibi for the time of either shooting, I didn't get the feeling that she is the person we are looking for."

"And the biological father?" Trevor asked.

"Still in prison."

I took a sip of my coffee and then set it aside. Woody was a fantastic person and an excellent cop, but he was a terrible coffee maker. "Before we continue looking at the files we found in Bryson's closet, I wanted to ask about the wife. At one point, you said she was a suspect."

"She was. And I guess in the opinion of some, she still is. Personally, while I guess it is possible that she hired someone to kill her husband, I sort of doubt that she's behind the man's death. If the shooting of the attorney existed in isolation, I might think differently, but with two shootings so close together, I have to think they must be related."

Maybe, but then again, maybe not. "Okay, what else is in those files?" I asked. "If it was Bryson's spirit who was responsible for the shoebox falling from the shelf, then the answer must be in there somewhere."

Woody took a few minutes to read the next file before responding. "This second file relates to a woman who has three children by three different men. The children are spaced about a year apart. It doesn't appear that any of the fathers are in the picture. The mother was homeless for a while, so the paternal grandmother of the oldest child agreed to take in all three children, but she refused to take in the mother. The children have lived with her for three years, but in those three years, the mother has managed to find a job and an apartment. While she voluntarily allowed the mother of the baby daddy of her oldest child to take her children in, now she wants them back. The grandmother is arguing that, while she never did obtain legal custody, the children are better off with her because she can provide them a stable home and a certain level of financial security, whereas the mother cannot."

"Tough situation," I said.

Woody nodded. "I agree, but based on the paperwork, it appears as if this was a new case for Bryson. I'm not sure that enough time has passed for emotions to have spun out of control, and Trinity was not involved with this case. Since the children were not part of the foster system, a social worker has not been assigned to them. It looks like Bryson was assigned the role of arbitrator between the grandmother and the mother to avoid dragging the whole thing into court. While I will look into it further to determine whether there was more going on that meets the eye, I don't get the feeling this is the case we are looking for."

"I agree," I said. "What else do you have?"

Woody picked up and read the next file. We all agreed that the case contained within the file was fairly routine. It was the fourth file he looked at that gave us all pause.

Chapter 8

"Okay, so why would Bryson have a file relating to a murder case twenty years old?" I asked. I quickly did the math. "He wouldn't even have been an attorney then. I suspect he would have been in law school, or possibly his final year of college."

Woody frowned. "I don't know. The case involves a man named John Thornton, who was accused of and later convicted of murdering his landlady." Woody sorted through the file. "There is no indication that Bryson was involved in the case. If he had been in law school, he might have helped with fact-finding or research. I suppose he might have acted as an intern of sorts for the attorney handling the case. Or possibly he worked in the DA's office. It's hard to tell." Woody continued to sift through the documents in the file. "I can reach out to some folks I know and see if his name comes up."

"The DA we have now has only been around for about five years, so he wouldn't have been involved in the prosecution of the man. Who served as the defense attorney?' I asked.

"This case was before my time as well," Woody answered. "But it looks like Donald Ferguson was the appointed public defender." Woody looked up. "Ferguson is a district court judge now."

"Okay, so maybe something was going on about the way John Thornton's defense was handled, and Bryson was onto it," Trevor suggested.

"Are you saying Donald Ferguson killed this man to cover up something that occurred twenty years ago that he didn't want to be leaked all these years later?" Woody asked.

Trevor shrugged. "Maybe. The guy obviously has a lot to lose. What if he did something negligent that led to the conviction of Thornton and Bryson somehow stumbled across a piece of information that proved this? What if he threatened to tell what he knew and Ferguson had him killed?"

"Sounds like a stretch. A really, really, long stretch," Woody responded. "And what sort of information could Bryson have stumbled across? And better yet, why get involved? Even if he did know something, taking on a district court judge would be career suicide."

"I don't know," Trevor admitted.

I leaned forward, crossing my arms on the desk. "What if Bryson had a personal relationship with Thornton?" I asked. "I am assuming this shooting, as well as the trial, took place here in Cutter's Cove."

"It did," Woody confirmed.

"So do we know where Bryson lived at the time of the murder?" I asked.

"I'm not sure," Woody answered. "Hang on, and I'll see if I can find out."

Trevor and I sat quietly while Woody worked on the computer. After several minutes, he spoke. "It looks like Bryson's official residence was here in Cutter's Cove at the time of the shooting. It appears he lived and worked in Cutter's Cove during his summers while attending college in Portland. The shooting took place during the summer of what I assume might have been his junior or senior year. The trial took place the following summer."

"Where did he go to law school?" I asked.

"Salem, Oregon."

"Did he continue to spend summers in Cutter's Cove after he graduated college?"

"I'm not sure."

"You said that Thornton was convicted of shooting his landlady. Bryson didn't have the same landlady, did he?" Trevor asked.

Woody turned his attention to his computer. He continued to type in a string of commands. As we had before, Trevor and I waited quietly. "I'm not coming up with an address. I'll continue to look for one. Your theory that Bryson might have lived in the same apartment building where the murder occurred is a good one. Perhaps he even saw something. Or perhaps he knew Thornton and had inside information as to what really happened. I don't suppose that speculating about what might have occurred will do us a lot of good without facts to back up those speculations."

I sat back in my chair and crossed my arms. "Okay. Say that this file is what we are looking for. Say Bryson's death has something to do with this murder case from twenty years ago. If that turns out to be true, we just need to tear it apart and look for a motive. But if this case is behind Bryson's death, how does Trinity fit into it? Trinity would have been a kid twenty years ago."

"Amanda has a point," Trevor said. "It would be pretty odd if the two shootings weren't linked. I mean what are the odds that there would be two shootings within twenty-four hours in this little town and they not be linked. Add in the similarity of the careers each victim was engaged in at the time of their death, and the odds of them not being linked would be astronomical."

Woody bobbed his head around as he appeared to be gnawing on the situation. "It would seem the two shootings are linked, but how? And why were different weapons used? If the killer was trying to throw us off by using two different guns, why not use two different methods altogether. Like a shooting and a stabbing or a shooting and a bludgeoning."

"I suppose the killer might not have wanted to get close enough to stab or bludgeon the victim, but I get what you are saying," I responded.

Trevor looked at me. "How certain are you that the shoebox falling off the shelf to alert you to the files was Bryson trying to communicate with you?"

"Not certain at all. In fact, I would say that it is more likely that the shoebox falling is unrelated to anything else that is going on here. Having said that, the presence of these files in Bryson's closet does seem relevant."

"Other than the fifteen-year-old who is in the foster care system, I wonder if we can link Trinity to any of the cases represented in these files," I said.

"Again, I can't answer that with any certainty without doing some additional research. At this point, I think I should really dig into these files and fill in as many blanks as I can. We can talk again. In the meantime, how do you feel about another visit with Trinity?"

"Yeah, about that," I hemmed. "The last time I spoke to her, she died, so her sister has requested that I not come by again. I told her that I wouldn't. I realize that connecting with her is the best chance we have to find the person who shot her, but Carmen is more concerned that her sister lives than she is that we find the shooter. Not that she wouldn't like to see both occur, but given the choice…"

"Yeah. I get it. I would feel the same way. I guess we'll just keep plugging along and hope that at some point, something begins to make sense."

Chapter 9

When Trevor and I arrived back at the house, Willow and Henry had arrived. It only took a single glance to know that the four siblings had missed each other and were thrilled to be together again. I really hoped that a permanent solution could be found that would allow all four children to live together. Siblings were destined to be in each other's lives; separating them seemed wrong. Of course, I did understand how difficult it would be to find a single foster home that could take all four children. I knew there were times in life when what *should be*, simply wasn't possible.

"So what are you all doing?" I asked the group as a whole.

"Watching cartoons," Billy answered. He looked at Trevor. "Unless you want to play video games."

"I might be interested in blowing up a few zombies."

"I'm going to make a get well card for Ms. Rosewood," Aspen said.

"That's nice of you. I'm sure she will love to see it when she wakes up." Something occurred to me. "I remember seeing a note somewhere that said that you called Ms. Rosewood on the day she went into the hospital."

Aspen looked sad. "I didn't mean to cause a problem, but I was just so mad. I told Ms. Rosewood that I was going to run away if she didn't take me back to my brothers and sister."

"What did she say when you told her that?"

"She said she was working on it. She said I needed to be patient."

"Do you know where Ms. Rosewood was when you spoke to her? Was she at her office or in her car?"

Aspen frowned. "I think when I first called, she might have been driving, but then she got to where she was going. I'm not sure if it was home or somewhere else. She said she'd call me back after she got inside. I didn't want her to hang up until she promised to come and get me, but then she asked someone what they were doing there. The next thing I knew, she hung up. She never even said goodbye."

"Did she say anything else? Do you know who she was talking to?"

"No. She didn't say. She just asked someone what they were doing there and then she hung up."

"So do you think she was still in the car when she spoke to this other person?" I asked.

"I think she was just getting out." Aspen paused as if trying to remember her conversation. "We were talking, and she told me she would call me back when she got inside. I heard her moving stuff around, and then I heard the door ding when she opened it."

"Ding?' I asked.

"That sound a car makes if you leave the keys in it or the lights on. My dad's car is too old to make a sound, but my friend, Evette's, mom has a car that dings all the time."

"Okay, so Ms. Rosewood was driving somewhere when you called. She spoke to you until she reached her destination and wanted to call you back. You didn't want her to hang up, so you kept talking. While this was going on, based on what you heard, it sounds like she gathered her belongings and opened her door, causing a warning to sound. I think you might have been right that she left her lights on or left the keys in the ignition. Then what?"

"Then she said, 'what are you doing here?' I heard a loud noise, and then the phone went dead. I thought she might have dropped the phone and would call me back, but she never did."

"Did you speak to Ms. Rosewood earlier in the day as well?" I remembered that Woody mentioned a call from the house phone where Aspen was staying about three hours before Trinity ended up in the hospital.

"No. Just one time."

So maybe the foster mother had called and spoken to Trinity. I'd have Woody check it out. "Did Ms. Rosewood visit with you before you were taken from your parents and put in foster care?"

"She came by sometimes. She was supposed to check up on us, and she had things to give to my parents. Letters and stuff."

"And what did you think of her? Did you like her? Not like her?"

Aspen shrugged.

"You can tell me how you really felt. No one else has to know."

"I liked her. Billy said she was trouble and that we shouldn't be nice to her, but she was always nice to me. She even helped me with my homework sometimes when she came by. My dad said she should mind her own business, and my mom seemed scared of her. I guess I was the only one who didn't mind when she visited." Aspen looked toward the kitchen. "Your mom is baking something for dessert. Can I go and help her?"

"Absolutely. And thank you for sharing your thoughts with me."

After Aspen went into the kitchen, I poked my head into the den to check on Trevor and the other three children. Trevor and Billy were shooting zombies while Willow and Henry looked on. Henry sat on the sofa next to Billy and Willow was in Trevor's lap. Suddenly, I could totally imagine Trevor being a father. I had to admit that startled me. He'd always been somewhat of an overgrown kid himself, but as he'd been trying to tell me, and I'd observed for myself, he'd grown up during the years I'd been away."

"Do you want to play?" Trevor asked me.

"No, thanks. I just wanted to see how everyone was doing. Do you think you can pause the game just for a minute? I need to tell you something in private."

Billy scowled at me and Willow let out a little cry when Trevor put her down, but I promised the entire gang that Uncle Trevor, as they had been calling him, would be right back.

"So what's up?" Trevor asked after we were in the hallway.

I told him what Aspen had shared with me.

"Billy said something as well. I tried to slip in a few well-placed questions about Trinity and her time at their home, and he told me that she came by about a couple weeks ago to speak to his dad. He'd been outside playing in the backyard when she stopped by. He didn't want to get in the middle of an argument, so he decided to stay there until the social worker left. He was hiding behind a bush, looking through the window to keep an eye on things when Trinity got a call. She looked at her phone, said something to his dad, and then came outside to speak to whoever had called. Billy said she looked upset. She walked back and forth across the patio while she spoke to whoever was on the phone. He said she looked angry or maybe scared. He wasn't sure which, but she wasn't smiling."

"Did he hear anything she said?"

Trevor shook his head. "Not really. Or at least not for sure. He thought he heard her say something about Dyson or Tyson, but he wasn't sure. He said when she hung up, she hugged her phone to her chest and bowed her head. He thought she was crying, but then she looked up, took a breath, and went back inside."

"Could she have said Bryson?"

Trevor shrugged. "Maybe. Like I said, he wasn't really sure. I suppose it would make sense based on everything else that was going on that she'd said Bryson."

"I agree. Although I think we should bring up the names Dyson or Tyson to Woody as well."

Trevor looked back toward the den. "I'd better get back. Maybe we can talk about it some more after we get the kids off to bed."

After Trevor returned to the game, I headed upstairs to call Woody. I figured that he would be interested in both the chat I'd had with Aspen and the information Trevor had gotten from Billy. If Trinity had been shot as she'd gotten out of the car, and it had been the shooter she'd spoken to when she asked why they were there, then it sounded as if she knew her shooter. That wasn't a huge clue, but it was something. I also brought up the Dyson, Tyson, Bryson discussion Trevor and I'd had.

"I agree that she most likely said Bryson, but I do remember seeing a file for someone named Dyson in the case files I requested," Woody said. "Hang on, and I'll look for it."

I agreed to wait on the line while he shuffled through the paperwork on his desk.

After a few minutes, he came on the line. "Trinity was working with a woman named Rita Dyson. The Dyson children were taken from their parents following a report filed by the teacher of one of the children stating that her student frequently came to school with bruises on his arms and legs. Initially, both parents denied the allegation that abuse of any sort was taking place. An investigation was conducted, and after it was determined that the other two children in the family also suffered a larger than statistically average number of bumps and bruises, the case was assigned to Trinity and eventually the children were removed from the home. After her children were taken, Mrs. Dyson decided to admit that it was her husband, who as it turned out was not the biological father of the children, who had been doling out the harsh treatment. The woman wanted to have her children returned to her, so she agreed to enter a shelter for abused women. She received both counseling and legal aid, and Trinity was working with the court to have the woman reunited with her children in a location away from the stepfather."

"So maybe she received news regarding this case the day Billy overheard the conversation," I suggested. "News that appeared to have saddened or angered her."

"I'll look into it and call you back. It does sound like a volatile situation with the potential to have led to violence."

After I hung up with Woody, I walked over to the window and looked out. The sky was dark, but it wasn't raining. Maybe I'd take the dogs out for a quick walk. I'd just turned away from the window when I had a flash. In my mind, a man was standing on the edge of the forest watching the house. I turned back around, but couldn't see anyone standing there. Of course, the distance from the house to the forest was quite a ways.

"Alyson," I called.

She appeared. "Hey. What's up?"

"I had another flash. This time I saw a man standing at the edge of the woods, looking toward the house. Can you pop over and check it out?"

"On it," she said and then disappeared. A few minutes later, she reappeared. "There is a man. Dark hair, dark pants, tan-colored jacket."

"What's he doing?"

"Nothing. He's just standing there. I guess he might be watching you or he might be watching the kids."

"Either way, I'm going to call Woody back and ask him to check it out. Someone watching the house is not a situation I'm at all comfortable with."

Chapter 10

Monday, November 19

By the time Woody had arrived the previous evening to look around, the man was gone. We all had a theory as to who the man might have been and why he might have been lurking. The most logical explanation was that he had heard that the children were staying with us and had been here to confirm the fact for one reason or another. He might have been a hiker who ended up at the edge of our property line, or he could have been watching the house for an entirely different reason.

The person who had sent me the threatening texts a while back still hadn't been nailed down, and while Donovan suspected the person who sent the texts didn't realize I wasn't in New York, we really didn't know that. I supposed it had been in the back of my mind that the person behind the texts was eventually going to figure out where I was. If he was serious about getting payback for Clay and Mario's deaths, as the texts seemed to indicate, then it was only a matter of time until he found me. Still, I didn't want to worry anyone by bringing up the idea that the man watching the house might not have been here to confirm the presence of the children, and since everyone seemed to assume that was true, I decided not to offer the alternate theory.

Trevor didn't want to leave my mom, the kids, and me alone in the house, so he volunteered to stay overnight again. Since the four children were using both guest rooms, Trevor had offered to sleep on the sofa. I wasn't sure what was going to happen in the long run, but I supposed we'd just take each hour and each day as they came.

When Woody and I had spoken the previous evening, he'd indicated that he planned to contact social services about a longer-term plan for the four children currently in our care. He hoped to find a responsible relative willing to take all four at least until something could be worked out with the parents. He also planned to continue to follow up on the leads we'd dug up related to the shootings. I really hoped we'd be able to get everything tied up before Thanksgiving, but it wasn't looking that way.

Pirates Pizza, the restaurant Trevor owned, was closed on Mondays, so he planned to spend the day helping us to do whatever we needed help doing. I wasn't sure if Mac and Ty were returning today or tomorrow, but I supposed we'd hear from them one way or another in the next day or two. According to Mom, Donovan planned to arrive in Cutter's Cove on Tuesday evening. He was going to fly into Portland

and rent a car. I knew he'd booked a room at one of the inns along the coast, so I doubted we'd see him until Wednesday. I was really looking forward to catching up with him.

The kids were out of school for the holiday this week and seemed content to watch cartoons this morning, while Mom seemed happy to tackle the pies she planned to bake in anticipation of Thanksgiving, so Trevor and I decided to take the dogs for a walk. The storm had blown through, and the sky was blue this morning, although, according to the weather forecast, there was another storm due to blow in by Wednesday.

"I never get tired of this," I said, as we strolled along the bluff with the dogs. I found that the rhythm of the waves crashing on the rocks below created a serene atmosphere that instantly drove away any residual stress I might be hanging onto.

"So what is your plan for today?" Trevor asked.

"I'm going to start by calling Woody to see if he has any updates, and then I thought I'd talk to Mom about what she needs to have done in preparation for Thursday. I know she is all over the baking and whatnot, but I thought I'd offer to tackle the grocery shopping. It's a real challenge each year. I figured I'd go tomorrow unless something comes up between now and then." I slowed to let Tucker, who had begun to lag, catch up. "I also wanted to explore these flashes I've been having. I don't know where they come from or what they mean. At this point, I can't really control them, and I don't even know what they are. I guess seeing Bryson being shot before it happened was a premonition of some sort, but then seeing the man in the forest last night was an insight that felt like it came to me in real-time."

"What do you mean by 'explore these flashes?'" Trevor asked.

I shrugged. "I'm not exactly sure. I guess I want to see if I can conjure up an image by focusing on someone or something. I really have no idea how it works or why it is happening now, but if I could conjure up an image on demand, I think that would come in pretty darn useful."

Trevor wove his fingers through mine. "I suppose it would be useful, but it also seems that having these flashes popping into your head on any sort of a regular basis would be extremely stressful as well."

"I suppose that's true. Still, if I could conjure up an image of Trinity being shot, I would be able to know who shot her."

"I suppose." Trevor frowned.

My phone dinged. I pulled it out of my pocket. "It's a text from Mac. She says they are having a fabulous time and will be home tomorrow. Ty will be coming to Cutter's Cove with her and plans to stay through the Thanksgiving weekend."

"I'm glad things are working out for the two of them. They seem really good together."

"I agree. Although I'm really going to miss Mac if she moves to Portland to be closer to Ty."

Trevor tightened his fingers around mine. "If I know Mac, and I do, she will take her time in making a decision like that. I've no doubt that the two will be back and forth pretty much every weekend so they can spend time together, but Mac isn't the sort to rush into things."

"Yeah. I guess you're right."

"We should head back," Trevor suggested. "I hate to leave your mom with all the kids for too long."

"I doubt she minds, but I think Tucker is getting tired." I stopped and called to Sunny, who'd run ahead a bit. She turned and headed toward us. Once she arrived, Trevor and I turned around and headed back toward the house. "I've been thinking about something Billy said when we were looking for Aspen. He said that they had a place they'd go to when they needed to hide. I've wondered ever since then what, or more likely who, the children felt they needed to hide from."

"Yeah, I've been wondering the same thing," Trevor said. "My immediate thought was that they needed to hide from one or both of their parents at times. The thing is that all the kids seem to be missing their mother and father, and I'm not picking up a fear or abuse vibe at all. Sure, the parents were negligent in that they left the kids alone without adult supervision, but no one has mentioned them being drunk, angry, or violent in any way. It makes me wonder if it wasn't someone else they felt that had to hide from."

"If there is someone else, I wonder who it is?"

"I don't know. Perhaps a friend or neighbor with abusive tendencies. I'm going to try gently broaching the subject with Billy during the video game session I promised him when I get back to the house. Maybe he'll let something slip."

"That's a good idea. I can see that all the kids adore you. Maybe if they get comfortable enough, they will be willing to share what they know."

By the time we returned, all the kids were waiting for Trevor in the den. He went to play with them while I went upstairs to speak to Woody. He'd had a lot of leads to follow up on, and I wondered if he'd made progress on any of them.

"I do have a few things to share," Woody said after I called and asked him for an update. "First of all, Bryson's wife has been formally cleared of all suspicion in the death of her husband. I guess the detective assigned to the case has looked into the situation extensively and is convinced that she is not the person we are looking for."

"I guess that is one less person on the suspect list."

"Actually, there are several fewer people on the list. In addition to Bryson's wife being removed, Devon Long's mother has been cleared as well. I guess she was meeting with her parole officer at the time Bryson was shot."

"Devon Long is the fifteen-year-old in foster care."

"Yes, that is correct. Apparently, before he died, Bryson had negotiated a deal between the mother and the foster parents where she would legally allow the foster parents to adopt Devon in return for visitation. The paperwork hadn't been submitted as of the time of Bryson's death, but the detective in charge of the case has spoken to all the involved parties, and everyone seems to want what is best for the boy."

"So it is unlikely that anyone involved in the case had anything to do with Trinity's shooting either."

"Very unlikely," Woody confirmed.

"You said there were several suspects eliminated."

"We spoke about a case involving a woman who had three children fathered by three different men.

The grandmother of the oldest child has been raising all three for the past three years, but in those three years, the mother has gotten her act together and has a job and a place to live. The grandmother was balking about returning the children to their mother, but it seems that, with Bryson's help, the mother and grandmother worked out a compromise for a shared custody arrangement. The children will continue to live with the grandmother when school is in session, and the mother will be allowed to have the children with her on alternate weekends and during summer vacation. It's really a lot like a custody arrangement between divorced parents. I will admit that this is a bit more complicated, but it seems that everyone is happy, at least for the time being. I spoke to both the mother and grandmother, and they seemed to feel that Bryson had done a good job finding a solution they could both live with."

"So who does that leave?" I asked.

"There aren't a lot of suspects left. I have spoken to the mother of the four children currently residing in your home. I have no reason to believe she had anything to do with any of this. As I've said before, she genuinely seems to love her children. She was just overworked and overwhelmed and made some bad choices. I spoke to Leslie, the social worker assigned to take over the case from Trinity, and she agrees that the mother of the children really had no motive to shoot Trinity or Bryson. The father couldn't have done it since he was in custody during the shootings, so it seems they are both off the list as well, although neither was ever actually on my list."

"Any luck finding a relative to take them?"

"A relative no, but there is a friend of the family, a woman named Silvia Brown, who is currently living in Salem, Oregon and has expressed an interest in taking all four children into her home. She was friends with the children's mother when they were kids and has kept in touch with the family. Leslie is looking into the possibility, and it is looking good at this point. The children's mother has made plans to move as well if Ms. Brown's request is approved. Of course, with the holiday this week, things move slowly, but given the situation, I wouldn't be surprised if a temporary arrangement isn't worked out by the end of the day. I guess we'll see what happens. Hang on."

I could hear talking in the background, although I couldn't hear what was being said.

"I'm sorry, but I need to go. Can I call you back later?"

"Absolutely," I replied.

After I hung up with Woody, I went back downstairs. The kids seemed happy with Trevor, so I headed into the kitchen to chat with Mom about the upcoming holiday. The kitchen smelled wonderful. I always had loved it when Mom baked.

"Trevor and I spoke about going to the grocery store early in the morning before it gets too crowded," I informed Mom. "I thought we could make a list today."

Mom picked a notepad off the counter. "I have a list started. I'm still trying to figure out quantities. I know you and Trevor, and Mac and Ty, and Donovan and I will be here. You said you invited Woody. Is he bringing anyone?"

"Not that I know of, but I suppose I should have offered him that option. I'll ask him the next time I speak to him."

"And what about the children? Will they still be here?"

"I'm not sure. Woody said the social worker who took over the case is working with a family friend who has expressed interest in taking in all four children, but he wasn't sure how quickly things would move given the fact that this was a holiday week. I think we should plan on them being here them just in case."

Mom nodded. "Was there anyone else you invited or plan to invite?"

"Nope. That should do it. Let's plan for eight adults and four kids at this point. If we don't end up with that many, I'm sure someone will eat the leftovers."

"The leftovers are the best part," Mom agreed. "Did Woody have any news about the man you saw watching the house?"

"No. And, unless he returns, which he probably won't, I'm not sure we'll ever know who he was. It was all pretty random. I mean, we don't really know why he was there. He could simply have been a hiker who came across the house and paused to take a look. It is a pretty awesome house."

"It is an awesome house, but I wasn't born yesterday, and I don't think either of us really believes the guy was simply out hiking and you just happened to catch a glimpse of him while he was looking toward the house. How did you catch a glimpse of him?" she asked. "The woods are pretty far from the house. It seems like you would have needed to have binoculars to see someone standing in the tree line."

"I guess it was more that I sensed him, so I sent Alyson to confirm he was there. Please don't worry about this. I'm sure we'll all be fine."

"Is Trevor staying again tonight?"

I could tell that Mom hoped he would. "I think he might be. I'll ask him. So about this grocery list."

Chapter 11

Mom realized she was low on sugar, so I volunteered to run to the store. I didn't want to interrupt the videogame war going on in the den, so I didn't ask Trevor to come along. My plan when I left the house was to head straight into town, pick up the sugar, and then head straight back to the house. I really had no idea how I ended up at the courthouse, but that was exactly where I found myself. It appeared that court had been canceled for the entire week since there were very few people lingering in the area.

I really wasn't sure what sort of information I hoped to acquire by returning to the scene of Bryson Teller's murder. I'd already established that his spirit wasn't hanging around, and I sincerely doubted that some random person would wander up claiming that they had seen the whole thing and had been waiting for me to come back so they could tell me exactly what had happened. Still, I found myself inexplicably drawn to the place.

Once I'd parked along the street, I got out and approached the steps where Bryson had died. I stood in the approximate location where he'd been standing when he died and looked toward the building across the street. I knew the crime scene guys had gone over the place with a fine-tooth comb after I'd given Woody the heads up about the fourth story office. I also knew they hadn't found anything they considered to be relevant to the shooting.

I tried to picture the event in my mind. Court had recently let out. There must have been a fair number of people still in the area when Bryson left the building. I closed my eyes and imagined the steps that I stood on littered with people. I pictured Bryson was dressed in a suit and most likely carrying a briefcase. The person who shot the family law attorney must have been a heck of a good shot to be able to put a bullet directly into his chest from an open window four stories up and across the street.

I opened my eyes and looked around once again. Picking out a single individual from amongst a crowd would be tricky. It seemed as if it would take a pro. I supposed the killer could have been a hired gun. If that were true, then anyone with the financial means to do so could have hired him. But if the individual who wanted Bryson dead acted personally, the list of suspects would have to be whittled down to very few people indeed.

I supposed that someone who had military training might have accomplished the task. I didn't know a lot about guns or sharpshooting, but I supposed a seasoned big game hunter might have had the skill necessary to carry out the task. But the parents of most of the kids Bryson was working with would never have been able to pull off what had been pulled off on the day Bryson had died.

Maybe Bryson's death had nothing to do with his job. Because of the link with Trinity and the fact that both worked in the area of family law, it was natural to conclude that the person responsible for both shootings would be found from within their case files. It was also briefly discussed that the cases might not be linked, but what no one had mentioned, at least anyone that I knew of, was the possibility that the two victims might have something in common other than their jobs. Perhaps they went to the same gym or attended the same church. Perhaps they'd gone to the same college or frequented the same conferences or conventions. There were dozens of ways two people could be linked, and just one of those ways was to have clients in common.

Of course, the handgun versus the sniper rifle dichotomy still led me to return to the possibility that the two weren't linked at all.

A man dressed in slacks and a polo shirt came out of the building. He wasn't dressed like an attorney, but he did look like he belonged. He walked over to the side of the building and took out a cigarette. Leaning his back against the wall, he took out his phone and appeared to be checking messages while he smoked. Once he was done, he tossed the butt on the ground, stomped it out, and headed back into the building.

What was it with people who couldn't dispose of their trash? There was a trashcan ten feet away from where the man had stood. I walked over to the cigarette butt and picked it up. As soon as I touched it, I had a vision of a man doing the same thing the man I'd been watching had done. He'd tossed his cigarette on the ground, stomped it out, and left it where it landed. The man in my vision, however, had been standing next to a huge gun that was mounted to a tripod type support.

I glanced at the building across the street. I hadn't actually been inside the empty office on the fourth floor where Trevor, Alyson, and I felt the shooter had been stationed. Suddenly, the urge to take a look around was almost overwhelming.

I hated to bother Woody, but I wasn't sure how I was going to get inside without him coming with a key. Deciding to check out the situation ahead of time, I crossed the street and entered the lobby on the ground level. There were six offices on the first floor, including a dentist, a law firm, an insurance company, a real estate office, an accountant, and a chiropractor. Deciding to take a chance on the realty office, I headed in that direction.

"Can I help you?" A pleasant-looking woman asked.

"I'm interested in the empty office on the fourth floor. I was wondering if there was someone with a key. I'd like to take a quick peek before I go to all the trouble of filling out an application."

"Actually, our office is handling the lease. I'd be happy to show you around. Hang on, and I'll grab a key."

The office, as Alyson had indicated, was very dusty, although, by this point, there were all sorts of footprints on the floor. There was very little furniture in the room, but it looked as if what there was had been moved.

"As you can see, this office has been empty for quite a while. I'm not sure why. It's a nice enough office, although it is small. What exactly did you want to use it for?"

"A bookkeeping service," I improvised.

"That should work as you will probably have only have one client in the office at a time."

I walked over and looked out the window. The line of sight to the courthouse steps was perfect. I ran my finger along the sill. It had been wiped clean. "It looks like someone started to clean."

"I guess you heard that a man was killed across the street last week. The crime scene guys were looking around in here. I told them that there was no way that someone snuck into the office, shot a man, and left again without anyone seeing him, but they insisted that it appeared as if the shot could have been fired from here. Personally, I think they were mistaken, but you can't tell those guys anything."

I looked toward the few pieces of furniture in the room. "Does the furniture come with the office?"

"Sure, if you want it. It's pretty old and beat up though."

I walked over to an old desk and began opening and closing drawers. Then I bent down as if to look beneath the desk. This allowed me to get a better look at the floor. I was about to give up and call Woody after all when I noticed something on the floor beneath the drape that hung to almost to the floor. I stood up and walked in that direction.

"What about the drapes?" I asked.

"You want the drapes? They are really in pretty bad shape."

I pulled the drape to the side. A cigarette butt laid on the floor. It didn't necessarily belong to the shooter, but given the vision I'd had, I wasn't leaving without it. I wondered why the crime scene guys hadn't found it. I guess it wasn't obvious unless you were down close to the floor. I pulled my sleeve over my hand so as not to disturb any DNA that might be on the butt and then slipped it into my jacket pocket.

"I'll need to consider things before I decide on the office. Can you tell me if anyone else has been looking at it?"

"There was one guy. Tall, dark, and handsome. He was an older guy, but very distinguished. He said he was interested in using the space for a PI office. I was surprised at first, but he said he was retired from law enforcement and needed something to fill his days. I get that. My grandfather retired from the police force after serving for over thirty years and opened a dry cleaning business. Anyway, the guy looked around and seemed interested. He asked a ton of questions and took some measurements and a lot of photos, but he never came back. I guess he changed his mind. Too bad. He seemed like a real prospect, and this office has been empty for a while."

"Do you remember his name?"

The woman frowned. "He didn't say. Come to think of it, you haven't said either."

"My name is Amanda. And you are?"

"Celeste. Celeste Berg."

"Nice to meet you, Celeste. I appreciate you taking the time to show me around. I'll get back to you about the office in a day or two."

Once I left the office, I called Woody. Call it a hunch, but I suspected our would-be PI was probably the gunman we were looking for. After speaking to Woody, I called my mother and assured her I was on my way with the sugar. I figured that by this point she would have begun to worry because I was taking so long, and once I explained to Woody that pies were at stake, he agreed to meet me at the house rather than having me come to his office.

"It seems to me," I said once Woody had shown up, "that this man pretending to be a PI interested in leasing the office probably used the opportunity to get a general layout of the area, and I assume to set things up so he could get back in. Perhaps he did something to the door to keep it from locking."

"And you think the man who shot Bryson was smoking this cigarette while he waited for him to come out of the courthouse?" Woody asked.

"I think he was smoking a cigarette. I can't say for sure if it was *this* cigarette. But if you come up with a suspect, you can use the cigarette butt to prove the guy was in the office, assuming you can extract a DNA sample from it."

"I suppose the woman who met with the PI might be able to describe him in more detail," Mom said.

"Too bad she didn't think to get a name or take a look at the guy's ID," Trevor added.

"Even if she had asked for a name or an ID, chances are they would have been fake," Woody supplied. "Most of this makes sense. It seems reasonable that the gunman would have visited the office before the day he showed up to shoot his target. I'm sure there are a lot of things that come into play when making a shot like that. Angles, light, line of sight. I'm still not sure how he got a high profile rifle into the building with no one seeing him."

I frowned. "That is a good question. When you walk into the building, three offices look directly into the lobby. It seems that someone from one of those offices would have seen him access the elevator."

"Maybe he came back between that first visit and the last visit after everyone went home for the day," Trevor suggested. "Most of the offices in the building close at five or six. If he had a way to get back in, he could have accessed the office during the early morning hours and then just hung out and waited until it was showtime."

"That actually makes a lot of sense," I added. "It explains why Celeste didn't notice him when he returned, and it also explains how he happened to be there even though court let out early."

"Did you ever figure out what case was being heard or why court let out early?" I asked Woody.

"The case being heard had to do with a child custody case involving a woman who shared custody with her ex but wanted to move her son across the country. I don't think it had anything to do with the shooting. The reason court was let out early is because the second case to be heard that afternoon was delayed while the social worker involved gathered additional data."

"Trinity?" I asked.

"No, a woman named Wilma Barton."

"Okay, so it sounds like the cases being heard that day are probably not related to the shooting. It does make sense that the killer showed up before the offices opened and just waited."

"If the killer was already in the office when everyone showed up for the day, how did he get out of the building after the shooting?" Mom asked.

"I imagine once Bryson was shot, everyone in the office building across the street from the courthouse must have gone outside to see what all the ruckus was about," I answered. "It would have been easy to slip out in all the confusion. Especially if the gun was in a carrier that didn't make it obvious that the item was a gun."

"Okay, so what now?" Trevor asked.

Woody answered. "I'm going to send this cigarette butt in for DNA testing, and I am going to pay a visit to the woman from the realty office to try to get a better description. Before I go, I just wanted to let you know that everything is being done that can be done to have the children turned over to the family friend who has agreed to take them in. I don't think it will be today, but hopefully tomorrow."

"Don't worry," Mom said. "We can keep them entertained until you get the details worked out. I'm just happy to hear that the kids will be able to stay together. They seem to be really close. I think they have had to depend on and take care of each other for a long time."

Chapter 12

Later that day, I received a call on my cell from a woman who claimed to have some information I might be interested in relating to the shooting of the social worker and the children I was currently harboring in my home. I informed her that I was not the one investigating the shooting and that she should call Woody. Then she informed me that she didn't want to speak to the cops, and would just keep what she knew to herself unless I was willing to meet with her. I asked her how she had gotten my name and number, and she replied that she'd seen me at the hospital and inquired about me. Once she had my name, she claimed to have looked up my cell number. Here's the thing. Very few people have my cell number now that Donovan has provided me with a secure burner phone. In fact, other than Mom, Mac, Trevor, Woody, and Donovan, of course, I'd only given the number to a handful of friends who might need to reach me. I'd also given it to Carmen

Rosewood. I knew that the woman on the phone could not have looked the number up and must have gotten it from one of the ten or so people who had the number, but why, if she had gotten the number from someone I knew and trusted, hadn't she simply said so.

I figured there was a good chance the call was either bogus, or worse, a trap of some sort, but I'd always been the curious sort, so against my better judgment, I found myself agreeing to meet the woman at a location we'd both agreed on. She'd wanted me to come alone, and I'd wanted to meet somewhere public, so we'd decided on the bench in front of the gazebo in the park. It seemed like a safe enough place to chat.

Trevor had taken the two older kids down to the beach while the younger two napped, and Mom was still in the kitchen working on her pies, so it was easy enough to slip out with only a vague mention of running into town and being back shortly.

When I arrived at the park, I found a woman wearing a dark blue coat, just as she'd mentioned she would. I sat down next to her.

"I'm Amanda," I said.

"Gloria."

"You said you had information for me."

She nodded. "I live two doors down from the Jenkins family. I work a lot of hours, as do most of the folks who live in the neighborhood, but sometimes I poke my head in and check on the kids if I know they are alone. I don't know the kid's parents well. They really aren't around all that much, but I have chatted with them from time to time, and they seem nice enough. I felt bad when the social worker got involved. I know how hard it is to make a living in this town, and I felt like everyone involved was just doing the best they could. But then I ran into Uncle Milton on one of my visits, and my view on involving social services changed dramatically."

"Uncle Milton?" I asked.

"He isn't a real uncle. He seems to be a friend of the children's father, but based on what I can tell, the father doesn't actually like the guy. What I do know is that Uncle Milton is a real scary sort. The children are terrified of him and will take off and hide when he comes around. I really couldn't figure out why the father of these children would let this man come around, but after a bit of observation, it seems that he has some sort of hold over the guy."

"Hold?"

"I'm not sure what exactly. Maybe the children's father owes this guy money, or maybe he is linked to him in some other manner. What I do know is that Uncle Milton shows up every now and then even though every member of the family is afraid of him."

"And you think this man is involved in the shooting of the social worker?"

She nodded. "I think he might be. I'm not sure that Uncle Milton shot the social worker, but I do know the two met. I guess it was maybe a month or so ago. I'd noticed Uncle Milton come by and I knew neither parent was home, so I decided to pop in and check on things. When I'd first arrived, poor Billy was trying to get rid of the guy while Aspen hid in the bedroom with the younger children. Once the social worker showed up and realized what was going on, she somehow got the man to leave. Aspen told me later that Uncle Milton came back to the house after the social worker left and the dad came home. She told me that Uncle Milton was angry about what had happened and threatened to take care of the witch, only she didn't use the word witch. When I heard that the social worker had been shot, I had to wonder if Uncle Milton hadn't done exactly what he'd threatened to do."

I had to admit that if what the woman told me was true, this Uncle Milton fellow did make a good suspect. "So why don't you want to talk to the police?"

"I have my reasons."

I supposed she might be wanted for some past crime, or perhaps she was in the country illegally. I supposed that at this point it really didn't matter, so I decided to move on. "Do you happen to know anything else about this Uncle Milton? Where he lives? Works? Maybe a last name?"

She shook her head. "I don't know anything more than I told you. I'm taking a risk even meeting with you. I'm hoping you will take the information I have provided and look into things. I also hope you will leave me out of it."

"Okay, I can do that. And thank you. This does sound like a genuine lead. Before you go, I do need to know how you got my cell number."

"I told you that I looked it up."

"It's unlisted. In fact, you called me on a secure line."

The woman shuttered her gaze. "Does it really matter how I got the number?"

"Actually, I think it might."

"I don't want to get anyone in trouble."

"If there has been a breach, I really need to know. If someone gave you the number who has been cleared to have it, then we don't have a problem."

"It was Aspen. She called me from the house phone. I wanted to be sure to talk to you directly, so I told her to call me from your cell when you weren't looking. I just hit redial. Don't be mad at her. She knew I would be worried and wanted to check in with me. She wanted you to know about Uncle Milton, but she didn't want to get in trouble for being the one to tell. Please don't be mad at her. She didn't know you had a secure phone. Neither of us did."

"I'm not mad. Thank you for telling me how you got my number."

After Gloria left, I debated what to do. I could go straight to Woody or I could go home and try to get more out of Aspen and Billy. I wondered why neither child had brought up Uncle Milton to Mom or me or at least Trevor. It sounded like they were afraid of him, and it sounded like this man had some sort of hold over their father, so it made sense that the father might have warned the kids never to mention the guy. I wasn't sure either child would tell us anything even now, but I supposed if I wanted a chance to speak to them about the man, I needed to do so before the transfer of physical custody to the children's mother's friend took place, so I headed home.

I pulled Trevor aside and filled him in. We decided that I'd talk to Aspen and he'd talk to Billy, and then we'd share notes. Hopefully, one or both would be willing to share what they knew.

I knew that getting Aspen to talk was going to be tricky, so I decided to take her up to my room where we could chat about things while I fixed her hair. I'd noticed her fussing with it earlier and was pretty sure she was feeling self-conscious about the fact that her pigtails were crooked. I assumed she'd tried to fix them herself, but had limited success.

"Have you tried braiding your hair?" I asked, after taking out the bands and brushing out her long hair.

"I like braids, but I don't know how to do them. Sometimes my mom does my hair, and sometimes our neighbor comes over and does it."

"I met Gloria this morning. She seems like a very nice person."

Aspen smiled. "She is. She comes over sometimes to look in on us. She has a little dog who is named Taco. He is really cute."

"She mentioned that there was someone else who stopped by your house from time to time. A man you call Uncle Milton."

Aspen looked down at her hands which were folded in her lap. She didn't respond, so I continued.

"Gloria didn't seem to like Uncle Milton very much. She said that it seemed you kids didn't like him either."

"He is my dad's friend. Daddy said we need to be nice to him, but whenever he comes over, me and Billy take Willow and Henry to our secret hideout."

"Did you tell your parents that you didn't like this man?"

She shrugged. "It won't matter. I heard Mommy and Daddy talking. They don't like him either, but they still let him come around. I think my daddy has known him since he was my age. They aren't really related, but I guess they might have been friends."

"Gloria told me that Ms. Rosewood met him and didn't like him either."

"She didn't. She told my daddy that he had to tell his friend not to come over, but that only made him mad. I know they argued about it, and that made Mommy cry."

"Do you think Uncle Milton would hurt Ms. Rosewood if she tried to keep him from coming over to your house?"

Aspen drew her brows together. "I don't know. Maybe. I heard my daddy tell my mommy that Uncle Milton was not one to be trifled with. I don't know what trifled means, but I think it means that he might hurt you if you don't do what he says."

"I think that is exactly what it means. Do you know if Uncle Milton has a last name?"

She shook her head. "I don't know. He only started coming around last summer. I heard my mommy tell my daddy that she wished he'd never gotten out of the slammer."

"So he was in prison."

She shrugged. "I guess. Maybe. I think he did something bad, and I think my daddy did something bad too, but no one other than Uncle Milton knows about it. I think my daddy is scared of him telling the police what he knows, so he does what Uncle Milton tells him to do. He even gives him money. That is why he and Mommy have to have two jobs. That is why we can't all be together."

Okay, suddenly it seemed as if everything was beginning to fall into place. Aspen asked if she could go and watch my mom do the baking. She looked totally stressed out, so I told her sure. I waited for Trevor to come up to my room which was the arrangement we'd made. If what Aspen told me was true, maybe it was not only time to have another chat with Woody, but maybe it was time to have a chat with the children's mother as well.

Chapter 13

Woody wasn't in when I'd called, so I'd left a message. Trevor and I agreed that Uncle Milton sounded like a solid suspect and deserved a look. If the children's father had done something in the past that had the potential to land him in trouble with the law or someone else, that could explain why he allowed Uncle Milton to come around and do as he pleased. And if Uncle Milton was squeezing the family for money, that explained why both parents were working so many hours.

In addition to that, if Trinity had found out that Uncle Milton was the lowlife he appeared to be, that might lend a clue as to who might have shot her. It sounded as if Trinity knew her shooter, and it also sounded as if the shooter was someone she was not expecting to see, and not happy about seeing. Based on what we'd been told, it seemed as if Uncle Milton fit both bills.

"I don't think we should seek out Uncle Milton on our own," Trevor said. "It seems like a man with a badge and a gun would be better suited for that. But I do think we might want to try to talk to the children's mother. She might be more apt to talk about what she knows if the cops aren't around than if they showed up and started questioning her."

"If her husband did something bad, something really bad that would land him in prison if it is revealed, she might not be willing to talk to anyone."

"Not even if the safety of her children is at stake?"

"I suppose in that case, she might be persuaded to tell us what she knows." I had to believe that this woman loved her kids, and while she might love her husband as well, I hoped that if forced to choose, she would choose the happiness and safety of her children over everything else. Of course, I'd never met the woman, so I supposed I couldn't say what she would do. But the bond between a mother and her children was usually pretty strong, so I needed to put my faith in that.

Of course, I had no idea how to get ahold of the mother, so I supposed I'd have to wait for Woody to return my call before I could take any sort of action.

Luckily, Woody called back a short time later. After I'd explained everything to him, he agreed to set up a meeting between the children's mother and me and to look into the identity of Uncle Milton. Wanting to keep my promise to Gloria, I hadn't revealed my source for this information, and Woody had decided to let it go and not push the matter.

"I don't want you going to speak to the mother alone," Trevor said. "I'll go with you. I'll stay in the background if you want me to, but I want to be there."

I raised a brow. "Do you think the children's mother is a danger to me?"

"No, but it does look as if someone associated with her might pose a danger, and since we don't know if she has been in contact with Uncle Milton, I'm coming along."

"Okay. Hopefully, Woody can track her down. If she has two jobs, she's probably at one of them."

As it turned out, she was at one of her jobs. Trevor and I headed toward Mini's diner.

"Mrs. Jenkins?" I asked, after entering the diner and taking a seat in one of the empty booths in the back.

"Yes. Who's asking?"

"My name is Amanda Parker. Your children are staying with me."

Her face softened. She lowered the pad and pencil she held and sat down on the edge of the bench across from me. "How are they? Are they scared? Henry tends to have nightmares, and Aspen is prone to sleepwalking if she gets overly stressed."

"The kids are fine. They seem happy to be together, and my mother is spoiling them rotten. Aspen loves to cook with her, and Billy has been playing video games with my friend, Trevor. They are safe and happy for now, but I do want to talk to you about a few things we need to straighten out so that they can go and stay with your friend in Salem."

"Of course. I'm happy to help. I only want what is best for my children."

"Do you think you could take a short break?"

She looked around. The place was practically empty. "Yeah. A short one. I'll let my boss know what I'm doing. Just wait here."

I waited as she asked. A few minutes later, she returned and slipped into the booth across from me. "So how are things going with Silvia's request to have the kids stay with her for a while?"

"Things are moving along, and we are trying to accomplish the transfer in the next few days. Of course, there is a holiday this week, so it is hard to know when we'll get the details worked out. I understand that you plan to go to Salem with the children when they make the move."

"Of course. They are my children."

"And your husband? Will he join you when he gets his legal issues worked out?"

She shrugged. "I don't know. I guess that is up to him. He doesn't like Silvia, so I don't think he will want to come."

"That may be for the best."

She nodded slightly. "I suppose it might be."

"I understand that there is a friend of your husbands who comes and visits. Uncle Milton."

The woman's face hardened. "I don't want to talk about him."

"I'm afraid you are going to have to. Probably to the police as well. The children are afraid of Uncle Milton. I doubt custody will be returned to you as long as he is in the picture."

"Milton is my husband's friend. Not mine. As far as I am concerned, the world would be a better place if he fell off the edge into oblivion."

I supposed that much was true. "Based on what I've heard, it seems as if this man has information he is holding over your husband. Something that will cause him harm if revealed, so, in exchange for his silence, your husband has been giving him money and allowing him to come around the house."

The woman looked down at the table.

"If you want custody of your children returned to you, at some point you are going to have to cooperate with the police. They are going to want to know everything you know about Milton. Are you willing to provide that for the children?"

She hesitated. She took several deep breaths and let them out slowly. "I'll do anything I need to in order to have my children back in my life. What do I need to do?"

"I'm going to call Officer Baker. He will probably want us to go to his office. I know you are working, but I'll explain what is going on to your boss. It isn't busy, so they should be fine without you. Will you come with me willingly?"

She nodded.

"Okay. I'll make the call."

As it turned out, Milton was actually Joey Milton Winston. He'd recently been released from prison after doing twenty years for armed robbery. A man had died during the robbery, but according to witnesses, Winston had not been the gunman. The gunman had gotten away and had never been identified. Winston refused to give up his partner in spite of the fact it would have resulted in a lighter sentence for him, which I suppose at least spoke to his loyalty.

During the twenty years Milton was in prison, his partner, Jake Jenkins, met and married the mother of his children. He stopped drinking, got a job, and became a model citizen. He tried to leave his old life behind, and most likely would have, had Uncle Milton not been released from prison the previous summer after having served his time.

When he got out, Milton looked up his old buddy, expecting payback for his silence. The children's parents had both been working two jobs ever since. Mrs. Jenkins didn't know if Milton killed the social worker, but she did say that she wouldn't be surprised if he had. She shared that Milton was not happy that the woman was snooping around and sticking her nose in his business.

Woody felt that the set of circumstances leading up to Trinity being shot made Milton a good suspect and shared that he planned to bring him in. He suspected that the children's mother and possibly the children themselves could be in danger if Milton realized she'd talked, so he made a few calls and arranged to have both the mother and the children taken to the friend in Salem before the end of the day. Trevor and I agreed to accompany the woman home and help her pack for her trip while Woody tracked down Uncle Milton.

"I wonder if I'll ever come back to this house," the woman said, as she packed clothes for herself and the children.

"Would you mind if you didn't?"

She shook her head. "Not really. I love my husband, but he should pay for what he did. I'm sure he will go to prison for killing the man in the liquor store. I wonder if I'll ever see him again."

"It's hard to say. I'm sure that if you want to see him, arrangements can be made. Did you know what he'd done all this time?"

"No. Not until Milton came into our lives. When I met my husband, he was such a sweet man. He was a responsible, hard worker. He seemed to have a good head on his shoulders. I never suspected for a minute that he had a dark past. Then this summer, Milton showed up, and I hated him on sight. I could see the kids were afraid of him, and I didn't want to give him all our hard-earned money. It was then that my husband told me what'd happened long before I'd met him. Of course, I was devastated. But I also knew that Jake was no longer the same man who'd killed a liquor store clerk. I thought if we could pay Milton off, he would leave, but he just kept hanging around and asking for more and more. I felt trapped. I didn't know what to do. I eventually confided in Ms. Rosewood. I told her that Milton was not only harassing us but that he was also squeezing us for money. She told me that she would take care of everything. Now she might die because I didn't have the courage to go directly to the police."

"Are you sure Milton shot Ms. Rosewood?" I asked.

She shook her head. "No. I'm not sure. But she was shot within a day of my speaking to her about Milton's record and the fact that he was demanding money from us. I didn't tell her about what Jake had done. I guess I hoped Milton would continue to keep the secret, and Jake wouldn't have to go to jail. I guess things didn't turn out the way I hoped."

"I agree that your husband is probably going to prison. But once we get you moved, you and the kids should be safe."

"Do you think Milton will come after us?"

"I don't see why he would. I really can't see what he'd have to gain by doing so. All the same, it might be best to not tell anyone where you are until Officer Baker has a chance to track down Milton and bring him in."

Chapter 14

Tuesday, November 20

By the time Tuesday rolled around, someone from social services had come to accompany Mrs. Jenkins and the kids to Silvia's home in Salem, and Milton had been brought in for questioning. Milton made the perfect suspect in Trinity's shooting, but he seemed to have a pretty solid alibi for the timeframe during which Trinity was shot. Woody planned to hold him as long as he could so that he had time to dig further into his alibi, but when we'd spoken earlier, he'd shared that he no longer was quite as certain that we had our man.

Trevor had returned to his home the previous evening, but he still planned to go to the grocery store with me to pick up the items we needed for our Thanksgiving meal. Since he decided to close Pirates for the entire Thanksgiving weekend so his employees could spend the holiday with their families, he only needed to work two days before having five days off. He planned to help me with the shopping this morning and then go into work after that.

"I have a feeling we should have been here when they opened the doors," I said, after getting a glimpse of the already packed aisles.

"It wouldn't have mattered. I've decided that the key to holiday shopping no matter how well you plan is to approach it with patience and a determination to find joy in the task."

I dropped a bag of potatoes into our cart. "I guess crowds are part of the experience. Fortunately, Mom made the pies and the rolls, so we can avoid the bakery aisle since it is totally packed. She has the turkey and many of the boxed and canned items she needs. Let's finish up here in the produce aisle and then hit the dairy section."

"Did Mac say what time they'd be back in town today?" Trevor asked.

"She just said today but didn't specify a time. What time do you need to be at the restaurant?"

"I'm going to head over as soon as we are done here. My manager has covered for the past week, so I agreed to handle things today and tomorrow so he could leave early on his own holiday."

"You really didn't need to come with me this morning," I said. "I could have handled things on my own."

"I know, but I wouldn't have gone in this early anyway, and I wanted to do what I could to help out. I guess I won't see you until Thursday unless you want to come by this evening. I close at nine."

"Can I text you later? I need to see how this day ends up before I promise anything." I paused as a woman crashed into my cart. There was no harm done, but it did irk me a bit that she didn't even stop to apologize. Of course, she had her head down like she was heading into battle, so I supposed she might not have even noticed. Trevor was right, the only way to get through this was to slow down and embrace the insanity.

It took Trevor and me over an hour to pick up the few things on Mom's list, pay for our purchases, and then make it back to the car. When we arrived at my house, Trevor helped me to unload our purchases, and then he kissed me softly on the lips and headed back into town. I'd gotten used to having him around during the past week. I was going to miss him now that he needed to spend time at his restaurant.

"Any news on Trinity's condition?" Mom asked as we worked together to put the groceries away.

"No. I actually thought I'd stop by and check on things today. It seems to me that if her condition doesn't improve or change, they'll probably move her to a long term care facility."

"I just feel so bad for that young woman and her family. Based on what we've learned about her, it seems as if she really cares about the individuals in her caseload."

"Yeah," I sighed. "What happened to her isn't fair." I folded up our reusable bags and stored them in the pantry. "I'm going to head out to do some errands. I imagine I'll be back in a few hours. Do you need anything else while I'm out?"

"I think I have everything I need. Maybe some flowers for the centerpiece. If you just want to get a fall assortment, that would be great. I'll text you if I think of anything else."

"Okay. I'll grab some flowers. If Mac shows up before I get back, please have her text me. I'm anxious to hear about her trip. At least someone actually managed to have some down time."

After I left the house, I headed toward the hospital. I'd promised Carmen I wouldn't try to connect with her sister, and I wouldn't, but I did want to look in on Trinity and hopefully get an update. I greeted the woman at the front desk, who remembered me and waved me through, and then I headed upstairs. I didn't see Carmen anywhere, but Trinity seemed to be resting comfortably, so I poked my head in her room. I swore I saw her hand move, so I stepped inside the room. When she moved an arm, I walked over to the bed. "Trinity?"

She opened her eyes.

I smiled. "Good morning. I didn't know that you were awake."

She looked confused.

"Should I get the nurse?"

She closed her eyes again, but I sensed she was simply resting.

"I'll get the nurse." I turned and left the room. "I popped in to check on Trinity Rosewood. She opened her eyes," I said to the nurse.

"Are you sure?" the nurse asked.

"I'm sure."

The nurse called for the doctor and then headed for the room. When I arrived, she was talking to Trinity, who'd opened her eyes once again.

"Is she really awake?" I asked.

"It appears she is," the nurse said. "I'm afraid I am going to have to ask you to leave while the doctor is here."

"Of course." I looked toward the bed and smiled at the woman. "I'll check back later."

"Aspen," Trinity said as I turned to leave.

"She is fine. They all are. The mother and the four children have gone to stay with a friend living out of the area. They are safe now."

She let out a slow breath and closed her eyes once again. I hoped that meant that she was relieved and simply resting and not that she'd slipped back into the coma, The doctor came in, and they bustled me out, so I had no choice but to leave her in the skilled hands of the medical staff and go about my day as planned.

After I left the hospital, I headed toward Woody's office. I figured he'd have an update on the entire situation by now.

"Trinity is awake," I said as soon as I walked in the door.

He smiled. "She is? That's wonderful news. Have you spoken to her?"

"Not really. She'd just woken when I was there, and they herded me out. She did say the word Aspen, and I assured her that Aspen and the others were fine."

"I guess she must remember that she was on the phone with Aspen when she was shot." Woody frowned. "I wonder if there is something more going on than we know about."

"What do you mean?"

"I'm not sure. It's just a feeling. I guess all we can do at this point is to wait and see how things work out."

"How are things working out?" I asked. "Any updates?"

"Jake Jensen is in custody. He has confessed to killing the clerk during the liquor store robbery twenty years ago. Joey Milton Winston has been released, but we are keeping an eye on him. During the timeframe for when Trinity was shot, he was with a friend who vouched for him. Now that his buddy, Jake, has been arrested and he no longer has anything to hold over him, my feeling is that he'll move on."

"Does he know where Mrs. Jensen and the kids are staying?"

"No. Only a handful of people know that at this point, and none of them will spill the beans. I think they are perfectly safe until we can get this whole thing sorted out."

"Okay, so if Uncle Milton didn't shoot Trinity, who did?"

"I've been thinking about that, and all I've come up are more questions. We know that Aspen was on the phone with Trinity when she was shot, but if you remember there was also a call to Trinity's phone from the foster home where Aspen was staying earlier in the day. About three hours earlier. We assumed it was from Aspen, but when asked about it, she said that she'd only made one call to her social worker."

"So who made the first call?"

"Exactly. Since the call came from the house phone, I called and spoke to the foster mother, and she informed me that she had not made the call and was in fact at work at the time the call was made. I have verified this fact."

"And the foster dad?"

"He informed me that he was at work as well, and he assured me that the children were all at school. On the surface, it doesn't look as if anyone was home to have made the call, but after really looking into things, I've decided it is possible that both the foster father and the oldest son could have been home. The oldest son is in high school and gets out at two o'clock. The call came through a few minutes after three. As for the foster father, he is a UPS driver who works in the local area and could have made a trip home without anyone knowing."

"Why would he lie about calling Trinity if he had?" I asked.

"He probably wouldn't and most likely didn't. I was just making a point that it was possible that he could have been the one to make the call. It really doesn't make sense to me that anyone in the family would reach out to the social worker of one of the children in their care and then lie about it, but so far, no one has confessed to having made the call."

"Well now that Trinity is awake, maybe she can tell us who called and who shot her."

"That would indeed make things simpler," Woody agreed. "I think I'll head over to the hospital and see what I can find out."

"Call me if you come across any new information. I'm going to head to the florist to get the flowers my mom wants for the table."

I decided to park in the public lot and then walk up and down Main to pick up everything I needed. That seemed to make more sense than struggling with the traffic generated by the holiday shoppers who were out picking up the things they needed for the holiday did. The town was already partially decorated for Christmas. The orange twinkle lights that had been strung in the patio trees along the sidewalks on both sides of the street had been switched out for white, and the window displays which a few weeks ago had featured ghosts and goblins were now decked out with images of reindeer and brightly wrapped packages. I loved this time of the year. I loved slowly walking up and down the street, looking at the windows. I hoped the general store still featured the huge Santa's Village in their walk-in window like they had when I'd lived here before. As of this morning, Dracula's Castle had been removed, and a snowy landscape had appeared, but I could tell by the boxes that were stacked in one corner that the window artist, who happened to be the store owner's granddaughter, had only just begun to create her magic.

I paused at the holiday store, tempted to go inside in spite of the fact I really didn't need any additional decorations. At least not for Thanksgiving. When it came to Christmas décor, I would need to take inventory of what I had and what I still needed to buy. Still, the hustle and bustle of holiday shoppers did feel inviting, so I opened the front door and slipped inside.

"Amanda. How are you?" Chelsea Green, an old friend from high school who still lived in Cutter's Cove, hugged me.

"I'm good," I returned the hug of the woman who'd matured into a giving and caring philanthropist from the snobbish homecoming queen I knew in high school. "How are you?"

"Fantastic. And so excited for the upcoming holiday. Caleb and I are hosting my entire family this year. At first, I was terrified that I'd either overcook or undercook the turkey, but Caleb reminded me to relax and enjoy the experience, so I decided to do just that. I heard your mom is in town."

I nodded. "She'll be here through Christmas."

"I'll have to stop by and say hi. I always did like your mom. She was a lot cooler than most of the mothers I knew."

"She's the best," I agreed. "She even came early to babysit my animals while Mac, Trevor, and I attempted to take some time away to relax."

Chelsea wrinkled her nose. "I heard your luxury cruise was cut short. It sounds like it was a simply dreadful experience."

"It was." I shared the dicey experience Trevor, Mac, Ty, and I had gone through. Chelsea had shared a few dangerous experiences with me in the past, so I knew she'd appreciate the twists and turns we'd had along the way.

"Like I said, it sounds just awful. I'm so glad you all made it back safely. It's been a really bizarre few months."

"It really has," I agreed.

Chelsea tucked a lock of her thick chestnut hair behind one ear. "I guess you heard about the two shootings in town."

I nodded. "Yes. Trevor and I have been working with Woody to find the individuals responsible."

"Any luck?"

"Not so far," I informed her.

"I guess you heard the rumor that has been going around about how the attorney had been digging around in some old case, and that it was him being nosy that led to his death."

I narrowed my gaze. "Who told you that?"

She shrugged. "There have been a few people. My dad for one. You know he was on the town council way back when and he tended to know everything that was going on. He told Caleb and me that Bryson Teller had actually served on the jury that convicted some guy named John Thornton of murdering his landlady. For some reason, twenty years after the case was tried and Thornton was convicted and sent to prison, this Teller guy starts having doubts. From what my dad told me, the guy had been talking to others in the community who were involved in the case back then, and that he had been digging up a bunch of old files."

"So how would that lead to his death?" I asked.

"Dad thinks that Teller was onto something, and Thornton might actually be innocent. His buddy from the yacht club seemed to think that Teller had a new theory as to what actually occurred and that it was this new theory that led to the real killer offing him before he could tell what he knew."

I thought about the files I'd found in the closet. Woody was going to look into them, but I had never had followed up with him. I wondered if he'd continued to look into the John Thornton case or if he'd become distracted, as I had, by everything that was going on with the Jensen children.

"So what exactly do you know about the case?" I asked Chelsea.

"Not a lot. I was a kid at the time the woman was killed. I remember my dad talking about it, but I didn't pay a lot of attention back then. My dad and Caleb were chatting about it recently, and he said that a lady named Vonda Valdez used to own the Seafarer

Apartments down by Arlington Beach. The apartments aren't there any longer. They were torn down a long time ago to make room for the Arlington Beach Resort and Spa."

"I know exactly the spot you are talking about. The resort is very high end."

"It is now, but back when Vonda Valdez died, the corner was occupied by affordable apartments, at least they were considered affordable based on their oceanfront location. Anyway, I guess that this Valdez woman was a bit of a curmudgeon who tended to kick people out whenever she had a whim to do so and for some reason, she'd decided that this John Thornton would be her next casualty. John wasn't going to go without putting up a fight. I guess that over the few weeks following the letter to vacate the property, there were quite a few altercations, some of them quite lively, between Thornton and Valdez. During the afternoon hours on the day Valdez was found dead, several of the other tenants overheard Thornton threaten to kill the woman. Several hours after the altercation, the woman was found dead in her apartment. She'd been stabbed with her own carving knife. According to my dad, Thornton confessed to threatening the woman in a moment of rage, but he insisted that he hadn't killed her. After a long drawn out trial, he was convicted and sentenced to life in prison."

"And Bryson Teller, who was a twenty-something-year-old college graduate planning to begin law school, was selected as a member of the jury?"

"He was. I think he lived in Cutter's Cove during the summer, which is when the trial took place.

Anyway, according to my dad, it seemed as if the guy was having second thoughts and had decided to dig around a bit, and as I've already said, it looks like that digging might have led to his death."

"Is your dad currently in town?"

"Yeah. He's around."

"I'm going to share what you told me with Woody, but I'd be willing to bet he'll want to talk to your dad."

"And I'm sure he'll share what he knows. Just be aware that he's been Mr. Grouchy pants lately. I don't think retirement is agreeing with him at all."

I laughed. "Thanks. I'll keep that in mind."

Deciding to call Woody and find out when he would be available to meet, I left the store without taking the time to look around. I knew that Woody had planned to head to the hospital and I sort of doubted he'd pick up, but I figured I could leave a message and let him know I had additional information to share. While I waited for Woody to call me back, I decided to head to Pirates Pizza and say hi to Trevor. I figured I could have a diet soda while I waited for Woody to call me back.

"What a nice surprise," Trevor smiled after I walked in through the front door. There were a few early birds, but the place wasn't crowded by any means.

"I just spoke to Chelsea, who provided me with some interesting information. I called and left a message for Woody, who is at the hospital, hopefully chatting with Trinity."

"Trinity is awake?"

"Yeah. A lot has happened in the past few hours."

"I need to head to the kitchen to prepare a couple of to-go orders, but you can come along and fill me in while I make pizzas."

"I can do that."

During the next fifteen minutes, I filled him in on my conversation with Chelsea and my experience in the hospital. He asked questions as he spread pizza sauce and sprinkled cheese, which I answered to the best of my ability. We discussed several options, including the fact that Bryson really had been onto something and the real killer had taken matters into his own hands to prevent the family law attorney from sharing what he'd found. Of course, there were other options. There had been six files in the closet. If the shoebox which held the shoes which held the key, happened to fall to the floor while I was in the room because Bryson helped it to fall to the floor, then, the information in any of the six files could theoretically have led to his death.

"So you think Bryson knew who killed him?" Trevor asked. "I mean the guy was shot from across the street. Unlike Trinity, who seems to have seen her shooter, I'm sure he never knew what hit him."

"That's true. I suppose he might suspect who had a motive to want him out of the way, but I don't suppose he could have known for sure who killed him. Maybe he just led me to the files to help provide us with the clues we'd need to investigate the case. I don't suppose we should just decide that Bryson knew who his killer was and could definitively identify him or her."

"Yeah, his case might be a hard one to prove unless we can find someone who saw the shooter on the day he accessed the office across the street."

I thought about the PI who had looked at the space. I wondered if Woody had ever figured out who he was. I supposed I'd ask him once he called back.

"I need two large pepperonis and a double cheese bonanza," the young girl who worked for Trevor called through the window into the kitchen. "Extra sauce, extra cheese on one of the pepperonis."

"Got it," Trevor called back. He picked up a ball of dough and started to work it into a circle.

"I also need an order of spaghetti with meatballs to go, an order of blackened chicken penne for here, and a meatball and pasta salad for here as well," the girl said.

"Got it."

I had to admire the way Trevor worked. He was the only one in the kitchen today, and yet he seemed unfazed about having multiple meals to prepare all at once. He simply slipped the pizzas from the first order into the pizza oven, and then started on the to-go order of spaghetti. He had the sauce made and the noodles just needed to be heated in hot water, so that order didn't take long to get ready. I wondered how he knew how much sauce to make or how many chicken breasts or meatballs to prepare ahead of time. I guessed he'd been doing it long enough to have a feel for things.

I was about to ask if he ever ran short on items when my phone buzzed. I looked at the caller ID. It was Woody.

"Hey. I take it you got my message?"

"I did. I'm just on my way out of the hospital. I want to talk to you about your theory relating to John Thornton, but I'm on my way to pick up Larry Dyson. According to Trinity, she isn't a hundred percent certain who shot her. She indicated that the whole thing is still fuzzy, but it is beginning to come back. She feels it will only be a matter of time. What she does remember is that Erica Hammond is the one who called her from the foster home where Aspen was staying. Erica is the middle daughter of Rita Dyson, the woman whose children were taken from her and put into foster care after it was discovered that her husband, Larry, who is not the biological father of the children, had been dolling out punishment severe enough to leave bruises. Erica left school during her lunch period and went to see her mother. When she arrived at the house they all used to share, her mother was lying on the bed with cuts and bruises all over her body. Erica told Trinity that her mother begged her not to tell because if the people from social services found out that her husband had beat her, they would never allow her to be reunited with her children, which is something the mom and kids all want. Erica agreed at first, but the more she thought about it, the madder she became, so she went home and called Trinity. Trinity had visited with the mother after the call and was on her way home when Aspen called her."

"I thought the woman went into a shelter?"

"She did, but she started missing her husband. He'd told her how sorry he was and how he would go to counseling if she would give him another chance. At first, she did as Trinity suggested and left the man so she could be reunited with her children, but after a while, she managed to convince herself that she could have it all if only he had really changed this time."

"I think that is one tiger who is never going to change his stripes."

"I'm afraid I agree."

"So Erica's mother wasn't wrong when she told Erica that telling what happened would prevent them from being together."

Woody let out a long slow breath. "She wasn't wrong, but the safety of the children has to come first. The woman really blew it when she decided to meet with her husband after being told not to do so. Her actions have only proven that she can't be trusted when it comes to staying away from the man. I'm not sure what will happen at this point, but I'm pretty sure reuniting the children and the mother is off at least for now."

"So maybe it was Mr. Dyson who shot Trinity," I suggested. "It fits. He was angry that the social worker had interfered. He beat up his wife for agreeing to go into the women's shelter, thereby disrupting his life. Maybe beating up his wife wasn't enough to scratch his itch, so he went after the social worker as well."

"I won't be at all surprised if it turns out that he was the shooter. I gotta go. I'll call you later about the rest."

Chapter 15

Mac and Ty were at the house by the time I returned with the flowers. They looked both happy and relaxed. I was happy that someone had managed to carve out a small amount of couple time. I knew they had been trying to do just that for a while now.

"Your mom has been filling us in," Mac said after she hugged me hello. "Wow. Talk about a complicated mess. I'm sorry your plans with Trevor didn't work out."

"Yeah, the timing could have been better, not that there is ever a good time for two people to be shot, but the timing was particularly bad for us. Still, I was happy to help out, although I don't know how much help I've actually been."

"So catch us up."

I filled Mac and Ty in on everything I knew to date, including the conversations I'd had with Chelsea, Woody, and Trevor that morning.

"So it sounds like this Dyson guy could very well be the one to have shot the social worker," Mac said.

"It sounds like it to me, but since Trinity doesn't remember who shot her, at least not yet, Woody will have to prove it another way. I'm expecting him to call after he interviews the man. Hopefully, he'll know more then."

"If he is the one who shot the social worker, is there reason to believe he could be the person who killed the attorney?" Mac asked.

I slowly shook my head. "I'm not sure. I don't know of a link, but I suppose there might be one I am unaware of. I know the man I suspect to be the person who killed Bryson Teller actually scouted out the office we believe was used as the sniper's base a week before the shooting. I think that the Dyson children were only recently removed from the home, so I'm not sure if the timing of the whole thing really fits. Although it might line up okay. I'm not entirely sure when Trinity got involved. I imagine it might have been a while ago. I doubt the children would have been removed from the home overnight."

"If the two cases aren't linked, that is going to be just too farfetched," Ty said.

"I agree. Given the timeline between the shootings and the fact that the two victims worked in similar fields, it seems that there has to have been a single shooter."

"Maybe the social worker will remember who shot her once she has a minute to get her bearings," Mac said.

"I hope so. So tell me about your trip."

Mac and Ty grinned at each other. "It was fantastic," Mac said.

"Where did you go?" I asked.

"We rented a beach house down the coast. It was nice and isolated. No close neighbors. It was absolutely perfect."

"It sounds really nice," I offered. "I'm glad you were finally able to get away."

"We really needed the time to ourselves. Ty needs to check in at his office, so we are heading to Portland after I pick up a few things. We'll be back tomorrow and plan to stay through the long weekend. Now that we are back to work, we want to help you if we can. Just tell us what you need."

"I'm not really sure at this point. I guess once Woody is freed up, we can talk to him and then take it from there. If Trinity remembers who shot her, that will be half of the battle. If the person who shot her also shot Bryson and Woody can get him to admit it, then we're basically done. If not, then I guess we still have some work ahead of us. This case has been really different from my standpoint. We aren't dealing with a ghost, so I'm not really sure what I bring to the table. But I find that I do want to help. And I have had the visions."

"Visions?" Mac asked.

"I saw Bryson's death before it happened and then again as it was happening."

"Oh, god. That must have been awful."

I nodded. "It was. Although at the time, I didn't realize that what I saw in my head was real. I guess it would have been worse if I had known."

"And since then?" Ty asked. "Have there been other visions?"

"Just one. I had a vision of a man smoking a cigarette. This led me to the office where we believe the shooter set up when he killed Bryson. I still don't know how that bit of information will pan out, but I am hoping it will lead to something. In the meantime, I just keep looking for clues and then filling Woody in with what I find. I really think he might be getting close to putting this all together."

Mac headed upstairs to grab what she needed for her overnight in Portland, and I decided to take Tucker and Sunny for a short walk. I tried to walk them every day. It was important for Tucker's joint health to get regular workouts to keep everything strong and loose. Sunny still enjoyed a good hard run, and at times, I did take her out alone, but Tucker seemed much happier to plod along.

I loved the sea when it was gloomy and overcast. I loved the days when it was cool and crisp, but not so cold as to cut right through your outer layers. I loved the natural ebbs and flows of the beckoning sea and the tides that seemed at times to mirror my moods. There were times I felt joyful and energetic, and other times I was melancholy and introspective. Today I guess the best way I could describe my state of mind was thoughtful. When I'd come back to Cutter's Cove the previous spring, I'd come with the idea of staying only for a visit. I had a job I'd worked hard for, a fiancé I thought I'd loved, and a whole other life on the opposite coast. If not for the death of a man who'd meant a lot to me, I'm not sure I would ever have returned. Now here I was six months later, firmly entrenched in my old life, which I guess was technically my new life. I'd quit my job, broken up with my fiancé, and settled into the house where I'd lived for two years while in witness protection. I supposed that it should feel odd to me that this house and this place felt more like home than anywhere I'd ever lived. The reality was that Amanda Parker was actually new to the area since my time in Cutter's Cove ten years ago had been lived by my alter ego, Alyson Prescott. Sure, I suppose I could argue that Amanda had been there under the surface the entire time, but had she?

I thought about Trevor. I thought about how much he meant to me; how much he had always meant to me. Now that we were skating on the edge of deepening our relationship, I found myself pausing. Was I sure that Cutter's Cove was where I really wanted to spend the rest of my life? At this moment, I felt that this very special place was destined to be my forever home, but I had only been back for six months. Would I decide that I missed the busy life I'd left behind, and change my mind about making this move permanent? It wasn't that I'd hated New York or my life there. In all honesty, I'd loved living in New York. Still, once I'd spent some time in Cutter's Cove again, I knew I'd missed it here as well.

I supposed I should be sure that my life really was here before I took the next step with Trevor. I knew he loved the town where he owned a business and had lived for his entire life. I didn't want to make a commitment to him and then find that my time here had actually been fleeting and had come to an end. I wouldn't do that to him. I knew that I cared about him too much to bind our lives any more than they were already bound and then leave him again.

I thought about his kisses. I thought about the way he looked deeply into my eyes as his lips approached mine. Most men I'd been with had closed their eyes when they went in for the kiss, but Trevor seemed to look directly into my soul. Perhaps the discourse I was playing through in my mind was all for not. Perhaps I was already bound to him in every way that really mattered. Perhaps my leaving for the second time had never really been an option.

"What do you have there?" I bent down and took an object from Sunny. "Where did you find this glove?"

She barked once and then ran toward the edge of the woods. I looked at Tucker, who seemed to be doing fairly well today, and decided to follow. When we got the edge of the woods, where I imagined Sunny had found the glove, I didn't see any other pieces of clothing, but there was a small pile of cigarette butts. Cigarette butts with the same red ring around the filter as the cigarette butt I'd found in the office across from the courthouse. I thought about the man I'd seen in my mind – the one who'd been watching my house. Was the man who I believed shot Bryson Teller, the same man who had been standing here shortly after?

Of course, I supposed the cigarette brand might be a popular brand that many people smoked. I'd never smoked and really didn't know one cigarette brand from another. One thing was certain though, given the number of butts he'd left behind, the man who'd been standing here had been standing here for a while.

Pulling out my phone, I called Woody. A stranger lurking outside my home was not the sort of thing I took lightly.

Chapter 16

"I'm not at all comfortable with you and your mom being in the house alone now that we know for certain that someone was actually watching you and the man in your vision wasn't just a hiker passing through," Trevor said, after I'd shown up at Pirates Pizza to chat with him while he cleaned up for the evening. "I think I should plan to stay at your place until this situation is resolved."

"I hate to have you disrupt your life that way."

He began loading items in the dishwasher. "I don't mind, and I'll feel better being there."

I shrugged. "Whatever you want to do. Now that the kids are gone, both guest rooms are open, although you might want to stay on the second floor with mom and me. Once Mac and Ty get back, I suspect they are going to want their privacy."

"The second-floor guest room is fine. We'll stop by my place and get some stuff once I am done here." He shut the door of the commercial appliance and began scrubbing pans which had been soaking in the sink. "What did Woody think about the cigarette butts?"

"He said they come from a popular brand of cigarettes and that he had no reason to believe the cigarette butt I found in the office across from the courthouse and the butts I found on the ground by the boundary between the clearing and the woods were left by the same person. He is going to request a DNA test. He also said that with the holiday this week, he doubts he'll hear anything until next week."

"Yeah, I figured as much. Did he have any other news to share when you spoke?"

I leaned a hip against the counter. "He said that he spoke to Trinity again and she still can't say with any certainty who shot her. He said her health is continuing to improve and she seems to be remembering other things she couldn't at first, so he hopes given enough time her memory will clear."

"Did he say if she had anyone she suspected?" Trevor asked.

"Dyson is still insisting he had nothing to do with the shooting, but Trinity did tell Woody that he was angry enough to have done it. She shared that Dyson felt that she was directly responsible for both his wife leaving him and the problems he is having with law enforcement. He insists that while he did discipline the children, he wasn't abusive to them and suggested that perhaps they just bruised easily."

"That sounds like a crock."

"I agree. Even if he didn't shoot Trinity, I have a feeling his relationship with law enforcement is just beginning after what he did to his wife. While the children's bruises were enough to have them removed from his proximity, the beating to his wife should land him time in prison, so either way it looks like the guy is out of the way for the time being."

"I feel bad for the kids," Trevor said. "Their mom hooks up with this loser, and now their entire lives are in disarray."

"It is unfortunate," I agreed. "Hopefully, they will end up in loving homes where no one hurts them. Every kid deserves to have a safe place to grow up."

"So what is going to happen to the mom?" Trevor asked.

"I guess that is up to her. Hopefully, she will stay at the women's shelter and continue what she started. I really don't know if she has what it takes to get out of the abuse cycle she seems to be in. I would hope so, but there is definitely no guarantee. If she really wants to break the cycle, then help is available to her and I guess that is all any of us can really do."

Trevor dried the pots, put them away, and began wiping down counters. I supposed I could have offered to help, but he seemed to have a routine, so I decided to stay out to the way.

"Are there any strong suspects in Trinity's shooting other than Dyson?" Trevor asked.

"Strong suspects, no. There are still a couple of the clients she was working with that Woody has not been able to verify alibis for, but when we spoke, he told me he didn't have a strong reason to suspect any of them. As for the Teller shooting, he is taking a hard look at the court trial where Bryson served as a juror twenty years ago. Woody feels it is significant that the man was looking into the case again all these years later."

"It does seem like the sort of thing that might lead to a shooting," Trevor agreed. "Especially if the person who killed the landlady, assuming Thornton didn't, is still around. Keeping a secret like that might very well be worth killing for."

"I agree. Woody has gone through the file Bryson had, but unfortunately, most of the notes are cryptic in nature and don't directly point to the reason he thought Thornton might be innocent."

"I wonder why he even decided to look into it after all this time."

I lifted a shoulder. "No idea. I suppose that Bryson might have come across a new piece of information. Maybe someone said something to him, or maybe he noticed something while researching another case."

"Like what?"

"I have no idea, but there are a lot of possibilities. I suppose if that we are curious, we can look into it ourselves. I'm sure Woody would give us a copy of the file we found in the closet, and he can get access to the initial police report. It would be helpful if he can track down the court records and any information available relating to the trial. Mac is in Portland with Ty while he takes care of some things he needed to see to at his office, but she said she wanted to help. I bet if I call her, she can track down whatever Woody can't get his hands on." I looked at the clock. It was close to ten. "I'll call him in the morning. Between you, me, Woody, and Mac, maybe we can figure out whatever it was that Bryson figured out that might have ended up getting him killed."

Trevor washed and dried his hands. "That sounds like a plan. I'm done here. Let's head to my place so I can get what I need, and then we'll head back to your place. I need to work tomorrow, but other than that, I'm all yours through the weekend."

Chapter 17

Wednesday, November 21

Twenty years ago, Vonda Valdez owned the Seafarer Apartments near the beach. There were twelve units, each with a water view. The units were in high demand during the summer, but during the winter months, the demand for the beachside units fell off sharply. Vonda didn't believe in long-term leases. She liked to have the flexibility to move people in and out as the mood and demand for the units hit her. This made her a very unpopular landlady since she tended to double the rent when the weather turned warm. This caused those tenants who had moved in over the winter to see a major increase in their rent without notice. Some paid, and some complained. Those who complained were tossed out on the street without so much as a grace period to make other arrangements.

John Thornton lived in the Seafarer Apartments twenty years ago. He'd been staying current on his rent and even agreed to the rent increase. When he complained about a plumbing leak in the unit he was leasing, he was told that repairs to the apartments were the responsibility of the tenant. John knew his lease did not state that, but he went ahead and repaired the plumbing at his own expense. The problem was that Vonda wanted his unit for a friend, so she decided to kick him out anyway. John was not a happy man when the eviction notice was served, and several rather loud altercations between John and Vonda occurred over the next several days.

When Vonda turned up dead, there were a lot of people who assumed John was guilty. Not only had he publicly vowed to kill the woman who'd basically tricked him into repairing the plumbing in a unit she'd planned to take back all along, but he'd mentioned to several friends that he planned to get even with the woman for ruining his life.

John was arrested and convicted of stabbing his landlady with her own kitchen knife. He spent the past twenty years in prison, all the while maintaining his innocence.

I wondered about that. I wondered why he didn't just admit to killing the woman if he had. He'd already been convicted of the crime and was serving a life sentence. I mean, really, what did he have to lose.

I'd called Woody that morning, and he agreed to send me a copy of the file I'd found in Bryson Teller's closet. He also agreed to send me a copy of the original police report. As for the rest, the court records and such, he agreed to work on it. I texted Mac and confirmed she and Ty would be back in

Cutter's Cove by midafternoon. Trevor normally wouldn't be off until late, but he decided to close early today since it was most likely going to be slow anyway. I guess that was one of the nice things about owning your own business. If you really didn't want to work, you could simply close up early.

Once I received the items from Woody, I sat down at the dining table to go through everything. It looked like the actual murder investigation was pretty brief. The officer in charge found a bloody footprint on the victim's kitchen floor that matched the size of shoe John wore. John had scratch marks on his face which he said he received when he grabbed Vonda's wrist during the last altercation they'd had. He admitted that they'd argued; he admitted that it had gotten ugly, and he'd called her names; he admitted that she tried to slap him, and he'd grabbed her wrist; and he admitted that she'd then scratched his face with her other hand, but he also said that Vonda was very much alive when he left her apartment.

The detective was able to track down another tenant who confirmed the altercation earlier in the day between John and Vonda. It really had looked as if he might be guilty and there didn't seem to be any other viable suspects. So after a cursory investigation, John was arrested for Vonda's murder and eventually convicted.

Based on the files I'd found, it looked as if the defense attorney assigned to John put about as much effort into proving his innocence as the police did in trying to find an alternate suspect. If John was guilty, then I supposed justice had been served in spite of the negligence of those involved, but if he was innocent...

"It looks like you're busy," Mom said when she came through the dining area from the kitchen.

"I'm just looking at one of the files Bryson Teller had in his closet. Have you heard from Donovan? Do we know when he will arrive?"

"His flight was delayed due to a storm on the East Coast, so he had to take a later flight, but he should be here by midday. I'm planning on him for dinner. Will the others be here as well?"

I nodded. "Mac and Ty will be here this afternoon, and Trevor is closing early. I think if we have dinner around eight, he should be able to join us."

"I think eight would be fine for dinner. If anyone is hungry, I can throw together an appetizer. Have you heard from the children?"

"No. I'll ask Woody if we can get a contact number or maybe he can arrange for them to call us."

"It would be nice to confirm that they are okay. The poor dears have been through a lot."

"Yes. They really have."

Mom sat down across from me. "So are these files providing any information you didn't already have?"

"Not really. At least not yet. If Bryson Teller was shot because of something he'd found out about the case, then it makes sense to me that the person who shot him would be Vonda Valdez's real killer. But if that is true, then figuring out who killed Bryson will not be an easy thing to do."

"What about the other tenants who lived in the same apartment complex twenty years ago? I wonder if you can figure out if any of them are still around. It seems like if Vonda treated everyone the way she treated this John Thornton, then perhaps one of the other tenants is the one who killed her."

"Perhaps." I picked up the file that Bryson had compiled. "I seem to remember seeing something about the other tenants in this file. Twenty years is a long time. It seems likely that most have moved on, but tracking them down might be a worthwhile endeavor. But not today. Today, I just want to focus on getting an overview. I still think the man who looked at the office building across the street from the courthouse is the man we are looking for."

"Was he old enough to have been involved in whatever happened twenty years ago?" Mom asked.

"Actually, he was. The real estate agent I spoke to said that he was a tall and distinguished-looking older gentleman, who told her that he was retired from law enforcement and had decided to become a private investigator to fill his time. I don't know if any of that is true, but it sounded like the man was probably in his fifties."

"Were there any male tenants in their thirties or forties at the time the landlady was stabbed?"

I glanced down at the file. "Names and apartment numbers are listed, but not ages. Again, I'm sure this information is easily obtainable. Maybe I'll have Mac work on it when she gets here."

Mom stood up. "I'm going to run into town to take care of a few last-minute errands. If Woody is able to work it out for us to speak to the children, please let me know. I'd really like to be here when they call."

"I'll let you know. And just so you know, things are crazy in town, so plan on everything taking twice as long as it normally does."

"Will do."

After Mom left, I returned my attention to the file. I wasn't sure if someone related to the events surrounding Vonda Valdez's murder was responsible for Bryson Teller's murder, but it did seem as if Woody was running out of suspects. He'd cleared almost everyone from his original list. I think there were still a few suspects he hadn't been able to verify alibis for, but none of the suspects left seemed to be viable options. Of course, if someone associated with Vonda Valdez's murder had killed Bryson Teller, then I had to wonder where Trinity fit into the whole thing. Could it be that there had been two different shooters? It seemed unlikely, but it certainly wasn't impossible.

I spent the next hour reading the notes Bryson had left. He seemed to be focusing on what happened after the shooting rather than on the events leading up to it. It seemed that Vonda Valdez was not married at the time of her death, nor did she have any children. She didn't leave a will, so when all was said and done, the apartment building, as well as her other assets, all went to her brother, a man named Vince Valdez. It seemed that Vince and Vonda had been estranged for decades and hadn't so much as spoken to each other since they were both in their twenties, until two weeks before Vonda's demise when Vince apparently visited Cutter's Cove.

I turned the page I was reading over, but the note left by Bryson seemed to end. It felt like he had continued his notes on a second sheet of paper, but it didn't appear to be in the file. The file I had was a copy, and Woody still had the original, so I decided to head into town to see if I could find the missing notes.

Mom was still in town, so I texted Woody with my request. He was in the middle of an interview across town but replied that he would be back to his office within the hour, so I went ahead and headed in that direction.

It was cool and breezy today. It had been raining on and off for the past twelve hours, and while I generally enjoyed the rain, today it just felt depressing. I supposed my overall mood wasn't quite what I'd hoped given the fact that tomorrow was going to be my first Thanksgiving back in Cutter's Cove, but it was hard to maintain a positive attitude when investigating a murder and a shooting. Two murders and a shooting if you counted Vonda's murder, which it seemed, I'd managed to find myself knee-deep in the middle of in spite of the fact that theoretically the killer had been arrested and convicted twenty years ago.

The drive to town didn't take anywhere near the hour Woody had told me he'd need to return to the office, so I decided to grab a coffee. I guess the rainy weather had everyone thinking the same thing since the place was packed, but I didn't have anywhere else to be until Woody arrived, so I decided to get into line behind the woman who I recognized once I'd filed in behind her was none other than Trinity's sister.

"Carmen?"

"Amanda." the woman smiled. "How are you?"

"I'm good. How are things with you?"

"Much better now that Trinity is doing so well. The doctor said he is even thinking about releasing her today. He is going to do some tests to confirm a few things, but she has pretty much been back to herself since she awoke and with the holiday this week, he is trying to release as many patients as possible who have reliable adults to stay with them. I'm actually planning to bring Trinity to my house for the time being. I have a very comfortable guest room for her to continued recovering in."

"That is so great. Really." I moved one space forward as the line moved up. "I don't suppose she has recovered her memory."

"Not completely. She seems to remember most everything except who actually shot her. A doctor came in who deals with this type of memory loss, and he felt that she might be repressing the memory."

I frowned. "And why is that?"

"Trinity remembers that she knew her shooter. The feeling of recognition, which quickly turned to shock when she saw the gun, seems to be intact. What she can't remember is the identity of the person who held the gun. The doctor who spoke to us said her memory may return on its own, but that it is just as likely that it will never return. He suggested hypnosis, but I don't want to put Trinity through that at this point. Her primary care doctor agrees. We both feel that what she needs right now is to simply rest and recover. If the memory comes back, then fine. But I really don't want to push it at this point."

"I understand. And I hope for Trinity's sake that she remembers on her own. It might be easier than to have that suppressed memory lingering in the back of her mind. I know if it were me, I wouldn't be able to really be at peace until I knew."

Carmen moved up with the line. "I suppose you do have a point. It must be frightening not to know, but I also don't want to do anything that will interfere with the progress she's made."

By the time I got my coffee and made my way to Woody's office, he'd shown up. He had the file in his hand that I'd inquired about and showed me into the conference room.

"So what are we looking for?" he asked.

"There was a handwritten note which I assume was penned by Bryson Teller in the file you sent over. It looked like the notes continued to a second page, but there wasn't a copy of the second page in the file you forwarded me. Since you have the original file, I hoped you had the missing information."

Woody slid the file to me. "Feel free to take a look. Do you think there was something relevant in the notes?"

I began to sift through the pages of the file. "I'm not sure. There was a note about Vonda's brother. I guess she didn't leave behind a spouse, children, or a will, so her next of kin, who was a brother named Vince, who Bryson indicated she'd been estranged from for decades, inherited everything, including the apartment building. The building, as we discussed, sat on the corner of the resort that encompasses that entire block now. The sale of the apartment building would have brought someone a lot of money, even twenty years ago."

"So do you think that Bryson found out that the brother had something to do with her death?"

"I'm not sure. If he did believe that, then it probably would have been included on the second page of the notes. He did note that Vince came to Cutter's Cove for some reason a few weeks before Vonda was killed."

I paused as I found the handwritten sheet I was looking for. "According to this, Bryson found out that

Vonda had been presented with a written offer to buy her apartment building six months before she was murdered. She turned the developer who wanted to build the Arlington Resort and Spa on the block that housed the Seafarer Apartments down cold, letting him know in no uncertain terms that her building was not for sale. According to Bryson's notes, the developer sweetened the pot several times in an effort to convince Vonda to sell. It seems the other businesses on the block had already accepted the developer's offer, which was contingent upon his being able to get all the properties he would need to do what he wanted to do."

"So maybe the developer was the killer," Woody said.

"Perhaps. It appears that Bryson looked into several suspects, including the developer. He also considered that one of the other business owners who stood to make a lot of money as long as Vonda sold might have met with the woman to force her hand, only to have their encounter end in bloodshed."

"Did he come to any conclusions?" Woody asked.

I turned the page over and continued to read. "Not really, although he did say that he considered the brother to be a strong suspect. Not only did the brother come to Cutter's Cove weeks before Vonda died after not having spent any time with her in decades, but once he inherited the apartment building, he sold it to the developer within days."

"So it doesn't appear that Bryson actually fingered a killer?"

"Not that I can tell by these notes. That doesn't mean he didn't make someone very nervous if it does turn out that someone related to the developer killed Vonda and not Thornton."

"Yeah, I can see how that might happen. And if it was the developer or even the brother, they would have had money to hire a pro. It really does seem as if Bryson might have been shot by a pro."

"I agree that it is looking that way. I'll see what I can find out about the current whereabouts of everyone Bryson named in his notes. Some of these people might not even be alive."

"Okay." I shoved the file to the center of the table. "Any luck with any of the other cases in the files? I know we decided this case had the most merit, but we don't know that Bryson led me to the files in the drawer, if that is even what happened, so that we would find this case. It could still have been one of the others."

"As I said before, the other five files in the drawer related to the fifteen-year-old who has been in foster care since he was four. If you remember, his mother had recently gotten out of jail due to overcrowding and for good behavior, and wanted to regain custody of her son."

"I remember. It seems that a compromise was worked out."

"It was, and I don't think she is the shooter we are looking for. The second case involves the woman who had three children, all with different men. All three children had been living with the mother of the baby daddy of the first-born child after the mother of the three children had become homeless. She wanted to retain physical custody of the kids, but the mother wanted them back."

"If I remember correctly, a compromise was worked out there as well."

"It was."

"The third case involved the stepdad who was awarded custody of his stepdaughters after his wife died. The biological grandfather of the twins wanted to raise the girls, and at first, it looked as if he would be awarded custody since the stepdad had a spotty criminal past, but at the last minute, the biological father, who had been out of the picture, showed up and sided with the stepdad."

"I remember that, as well. It seemed as if both Bryson and Trinity had sided with the stepdad. That seems like an odd choice, but maybe there was more going on than we thought."

"I imagine that might be true. The fourth file we looked at was Vonda's murder twenty years ago and the conviction of John Thornton for her murder. We actually got held up there and never really discussed the last two."

"Maybe we should now."

Woody nodded. "Agreed. The fifth file has to do with the case involving Billy, Aspen, Willow, and Henry. I think we know what is going on with that case fairly well." Woody set the file aside.

"The sixth file has to do with eldercare. It seems that the three daughters of an elderly man with dementia cannot seem to agree about what should happen at this point. The man in question has assets. Not a lot, but some. It's mostly property that can be liquidated to care for their father should they decide to do so. The eldest daughter wants to put the man in a state-run facility where he will be given the care he needs without impacting the financial resources of the family. She is arguing that given his mental state, he won't even realize where he is, and it makes no sense to spend the inheritance she is certain he wanted to leave to his children on end of life care. She has stated on multiple occasions that if the man was able to choose for himself, this is the choice he would have made."

Woody continued. "The middle daughter wants to have her father put into a private facility which the family would need to pay for. It is her opinion that the assets he has amassed to this point should be used to pay for his end of life care. She is insisting that this is what he would want if he was able to make a decision."

"And the youngest daughter?"

"The youngest daughter wants to take him into her home, but she doesn't have a lot of monetary resources of her own and is asking for financial help to see to his needs. As odd as it sounds, based on these notes, it looks like the older sisters are viewing this play by the youngest daughter as a means to get more than her share of the inheritance. She is insisting that all she really wants to do is to ensure that their father is as safe and comfortable as possible during his final time on earth."

"Seems like a hot topic."

Woody nodded. "Yeah. It's a real mess. The three daughters aren't speaking to each other, but it doesn't appear that Bryson, who had been appointed as arbitrator, had taken a stance at this point, so I don't see why any of them would shoot him."

"Agreed. It really does seem that the file most likely to have led to his death is the one relating to the murder of Vonda Valdez twenty years ago."

"I agree, and after hearing about your research, I am even more convinced of that. Thank you for bringing this to my attention. I scanned the notes when you first dropped the files off, but obviously, I haven't taken the time to give them the attention they deserve. It's been a busy few days."

"I ran into Trinity's sister, and she told me that Trinity might be released from the hospital today."

"That's wonderful news. I don't suppose she mentioned anything else about the memory loss?"

"Just that Trinity remembers the event in that she knows she was shot by someone she knows, and that she was shocked and dismayed when she noticed the gun. The identity of the shooter is still a blur, but she met with a specialist who told her that she is most likely repressing the memory and it may or may not come back to her at some point. It almost sounded as if it was up to her to decide to remember or not."

"It seems she might be in danger unless she can remember. I'm sure the person who tried to kill her isn't going to be thrilled that she is alive and kicking and perhaps able to identify the person who put her in the hospital."

I frowned. "That's true. And now that she is being discharged, she might be in a whole lot of danger. Maybe we should try to talk to her again. Carmen didn't seem to want to put her through any more stress, but I don't think she has considered the fact that the person who shot her might try again to accomplish what he didn't the first time."

Woody decided that he should speak to Trinity alone. He felt that an official discussion between a police officer and a victim of a violent attack might go further toward getting what they felt they needed than a casual discussion. I didn't disagree. Finding out who shot Trinity was Woody's job, and I'd only become involved in the first place because he hoped I could connect with Trinity's spiritual self in an effort to find the shooter. Now that connecting with Trinity's spiritual self was no longer part of the equation, I supposed my role was over.

Of course, that didn't mean I could set the whole thing aside and walk away. I simply wasn't built that way. I didn't want to get in Woody's way, so I decided to work on the other case I'd fallen into and pay yet another visit to the courthouse where Bryson was shot and killed. I'm not sure what I was expecting to find. The killer was obviously long gone, but I guess with Mom in town, Trevor working, Woody otherwise occupied, and Mac and Ty out of town, I was feeling at loose ends. The courts were not in session this week, so the area was mostly deserted. I sat down on a bench in front of the courthouse and tried to clear my mind. Maybe if nothing else, I could get another vision. The one I'd had before of the tall man with the silver hair and the rugged features played through my mind. I wasn't sure what good it would do me even if I could get a clear image of the man since I didn't know his name or have a frame of reference.

And then it came to me.

I'd seen the man before. I closed my eyes and tried to bring the image into focus. I still couldn't be sure if the man in my vision was the same man whose photo I'd seen in one of the files that morning. I was expecting to conjure up a vision of this man with Bryson, but instead, I had a vision of this man with Trinity.

My eyes flew open. I needed to talk to Trinity, and I needed to talk to her now. By the time I arrived at the hospital, Woody had been and gone, but Trinity was still in her room. I asked if I could come in, and she agreed.

I explained that I needed to ask her a few questions, and she agreed to help to the extent that she could.

"According to the files we found pertaining to your active cases, in the case of Alton Brown vs Ben Billingham over the custody of Aurora and Connie Billingham, it looked as if you supported the decision of the girls' mother to allow their stepfather to raise them."

"Yes. That's right."

"Can I ask why? It seems that the grandfather, a decorated veteran, would make a better parent than a man with a spotty criminal record."

"Initially, I thought that as well, but then I did some research. It seems that the reason Maria decided to name her husband as guardian of her daughters in the event that something happened to her rather than her father is because her father is actually a stern and rigid man. After speaking to Maria's friends, it became obvious that she blamed him for her decision, not only to cut the man who had fathered her daughters out of her life, but to cut him out of his daughter's lives as well."

"I understand that Maria was living with her father when her daughters were born."

Trinity nodded. "Yes, that is correct. According to Maria's friends, she felt owned and controlled by her father during that time. He seemed to want to control everything about the situation, and would not tolerate any behavior on her part which did not coincide with his wishes. He even insisted on naming the girls himself, calling the names Maria preferred stupid and lacking strength."

"And then?"

"And then she met Ben, and he convinced her to live her own life and make her own decisions. Ben is a bit of a wild card, but he seems like a really good guy. Admittedly, he is immature, but he really seems to love the girls, and they adore him. After looking into the specifics, I felt that the wishes of the mother should be upheld. Bryson agreed." Trinity frowned. "You don't think Ben…"

I gave her a gentle look. "I'm not sure. But I think you might remember."

She narrowed her gaze, and then her eyes shot open. She put her hand to her mouth. Tears filled her eyes. "Oh, god. It was him. The last time I saw him, he told me that if I didn't support him during the hearing, he would have to take matters into his own hands. I tried to reason with him, but he was acting like a madman, so I left. When I arrived home on Thursday, he was there waiting for me. I was shocked to find him there. I asked him what he was doing there, and then I saw the gun. Before I could say a thing, I heard a noise, and then everything went black."

"Do you think he might have also shot and killed Bryson?"

She slowly shook her head. "I don't know. I don't think so, but I guess he could have. He certainly had the skillset to take the shot, and it does sound as if he can be rigid and unyielding when it comes to getting his own way. I guess I wouldn't be totally surprised if he did shoot Bryson."

"Whoever shot Bryson seemed to have been planning it for at least a week," I informed the woman.

Trinity frowned. "No. That can't be right. A random shooting based on the heat of the moment is one thing, but to plan to execute a murder so far in advance takes a real sicko."

"Are you sure the man doesn't have mental health issues?"

"He shot me just because I disagreed with him, so he most definitely has mental health issues. Still, I'll be very surprised if it turns out he was the one who shot Bryson."

Chapter 18

By the time I got home, Donovan was just pulling into the drive. "Oh my gosh, I am so happy to see you." I threw my arms around Donovan's neck and gave him a hard hug. There had admittedly been times in the past when I'd been less than thrilled to see him, like that time he showed up during my junior year of high school and whisked me away before I could even tell Mac and Trevor that I was leaving, but he had also been there for Mom and me during the most difficult time of our lives.

"It's been a while." He hugged me back. "You look good. Rested."

I laughed. "Hardly. Just wait until we catch you up. Come in. Mom is upstairs. I'll let her know you are here. She is going to be as happy to see you as I am."

Tucker trotted over, wagging his tail. He was a protective dog, but he'd always liked Donovan. I figured the dog was about as good a judge of character as anyone.

"I like what you've done with the place," Donovan said after we entered through the front door. "It is much the same as the last time I was here, but I can see that you've added your own touch."

"Now that this is my home, I wanted to make it mine even though it was already pretty awesome. If you want to have a seat in the kitchen, you can look out at the sea while I run upstairs and let Mom know that you're here."

The next hour was filled with catching up and laughter. Donovan really was one of the people in my life I considered to be of the highest importance. He might not be as close to me as Mac and Trevor, but he'd always been there for me when I'd needed him the most. During those first months after my best friend had been murdered and my life had been upended, I wasn't sure if I would ever be able to enjoy my life again, but Donovan had been there for me, a strong and positive force, and somehow he'd convinced me that everything would be okay.

"Any news on the texts Amanda received a while back?" Mom asked. I was actually surprised that she waited as long to ask as she had.

"No. But things within the Bonatello family have been quiet the past couple of weeks. The power struggle that had been going on appears to have come to a standstill. I think that those in power and those seeking power are just waiting each other out. My hunch is that if someone from the family had decided to threaten you with the texts, they have been too busy with the internal struggle to follow up with what they started. That doesn't mean you shouldn't continue to be cautious, and we will, of course, continue to monitor the situation."

"What about the break-in at Amanda's old apartment in New York?" Mom asked.

"We haven't found any link to Amanda or the Bonatello family. I really think the fact that there was a break-in at your old apartment might be a coincidence. There are multiple break-ins in the city every day."

"I hope it is that simple," Mom said, although she still looked worried.

"So tell me what you have been up to here," Donovan said.

I took the next thirty minutes to fill him in on the cases I'd been working on since returning from the cruise. He made a comment about me finding trouble no matter where it might be hiding, and I jokingly agreed. It did seem like no matter how hard I tried to stay out of things, I always ended up smack dab in the middle of whatever was going on.

I was about to segue into a discussion of my adventure on the cruise ship when my phone buzzed. It was Woody.

"I need to get this," I said to Mom and Donovan before answering.

"I picked up Ben Billingham. It took some doing, but I managed to get him to confess to shooting Trinity," Woody informed me. "He swears he only meant to scare her and the gun went off accidentally. I don't know if that is true or not, but I guess that is for the criminal justice system to figure out."

"And Bryson?"

"He swears he had nothing to do with the shooting at the courthouse. I'm not sure why, but I find I'm inclined to believe him. I did take a photo of Ben to the woman who told you about the PI who'd come to scout out the place, and she confirmed that while the men had similar features, he was not the man she spoke to."

"So there were two shooters."

"That appears to be the case."

"So who do you have left on the suspect list?" I asked.

"Really at this point, assuming that the information in one of the six files you found in Bryson's closet does lead to his killer, I really think we need to focus on the Vonda Valdez murder."

I ran a hand through my hair. "Yeah, I agree that it does seem the most likely. I'll look through my file again and make some notes. Maybe you can do the same, and then we can compare notes later this afternoon. The gang is all getting together for dinner if you want to join us. And Donovan is here. I want you to meet him. I think the two of you will get along fantastically."

"I'd like to meet him as well, and I'm not busy tonight. I was going to head back over to Bryson's home and take another look around. I don't suppose you'd want to meet me there. Just in case he is still lingering and has additional information to share."

"Yeah, I can do that. I can be there in thirty minutes."

"That works for me."

I explained to Mom and Donovan about my last-minute errand. I promised to catch them up when I got back. On a whim, I decided to take my ghost seeing cat, Shadow, with me. I also called to Alyson and filled her in. She was happy to come along and happy we were alone so she could ride shotgun this time.

Woody's car was already in the drive when Alyson, Shadow, and I arrived. I picked Shadow up and headed inside. Once inside, I set him on the floor. I looked toward both Shadow and Alyson. "Okay, gang. We are looking for a ghost or maybe something left or possessed by a ghost. The ultimate goal is to figure out who killed the attorney. Take a look around and if you sense anything, let me know. No hunch or flash of insight should go unchecked."

"I'm on it," Alyson said.

Shadow just looked at me with a look of derision, but I was certain he was onboard as well.

"Do you really think there is anything else to find?" I asked Woody.

"I don't know, but if Bryson Teller was shot due to something he'd figured out relating to a murder that occurred twenty years ago, then we are going to need a bit of magic to figure this out. Not that good old logic might be enough given enough time, but I'd really like to get this wrapped up sooner than later."

"Yeah, me too. The gang is going to be together for the entire Thanksgiving weekend, and I'd really like not having this murder investigation hanging over our heads. It seems to me that the brother makes a strong suspect when it comes to Vonda's killer. If the brother is the killer and not John Thornton, and he found out that Bryson was onto him, then he makes an obvious suspect in Bryson's death. I don't suppose you have a photo of the brother."

"I don't, but if you are thinking the brother and the PI who looked at the office across the street are one and the same, I doubt it. I did a video chat with the brother just to get a feel for the guy, and he is about five foot six and two hundred pounds. I remember you said the man who claimed to be opening a PI office was tall and distinguished."

"Yes. He was. I guess the brother could have hired someone to kill Bryson. He did make a killing when he sold his sister's apartment building to the developer."

"Hey, Amanda," Alyson called out. "Shadow is digging at the carpet in the bedroom."

I headed in that direction. I wasn't sure what the cat was pawing at, but it did look as if one corner of the carpet had been pulled loose. I pinched the corner of the carpet and pulled. There was a floor safe underneath the carpet. Newly installed by the look of it. I glanced at Woody. "Can you open it?"

"Not without the combination. I guess I can call someone at the district office to come and take a look."

"Don't bother. Donovan can do it. I'll call him and ask him to meet us here."

Donovan had been a field agent for the CIA before he transferred to Homeland Security. He eventually ended up in witness protection. I really didn't know his whole story, but I was pretty sure he could get into a commercially built floor safe. He arrived within twenty minutes of my calling him, and five minutes after that, he had the safe open. There was a document inside the safe that looked to be fairly old. John Thornton had filed the document with the court, asking that a new public defender be assigned to his case. He claimed that not only was Donald Ferguson not doing his best to find the real killer and prove his innocence but that he seemed to be using the information he provided to him against him.

"Donald Ferguson was this man's public defender?" Donovan asked. "District Court Judge Donald Ferguson?"

"Based on the information we have uncovered, yes," I answered.

Donovan thumbed through the documents. "It looks as if Thornton provided some pretty persuasive arguments that his case was not being handled properly. Do you know if he was ever assigned a new public defender?"

"He was not," Woody verified. "In my opinion, there seems to be sufficient evidence to support the fact that Thornton was arrested after only a very cursory investigation and convicted even though the evidence gathered really didn't support a conviction. I'm not sure why Bryson Teller decided to dig around in this all these years later, but it does seem like he was onto something."

"Do you think Judge Ferguson would have killed Bryson if he was negligent in the manner he handled Thornton's case all those years ago?" I asked.

"I would hope that wouldn't be the case, but he is running for state senate, and he has his eyes on a national platform. If Teller was digging around, even if he couldn't prove negligence, it could have hurt his campaign."

"Ferguson isn't a tall and distinguished man in his sixties is he?" I asked.

"No. He is tall, and I guess some people would consider him to be distinguished, but he is in his late forties," Donovan answered.

"He still might have hired the man who shot Teller," Woody said.

"Or one of his handlers might have hired someone," Donovan said.

"Handlers?" I asked.

"Once you get into the political arena, you tend to collect people who want to control everything about your life." Donovan looked at Woody. "If you will allow me, I can have someone quietly look into the possibility that Ferguson was involved in Teller's death."

Woody nodded. "Fine by me. If Ferguson is involved, this case might be above my paygrade."

"I'll be in town for a week. I should have a preliminary report back that we can look at in a couple of days. What I need from you is a copy of everything you have relating to both Donald Ferguson and Bryson Teller."

"I'll make copies of everything and bring it by the house later this afternoon."

I bent down and picked up Shadow. "Good kitty. I knew there was a reason I needed to bring you."

Chapter 19

Monday, November 26

"I think this tree will be perfect for the entry," Mom said, as she stood proudly in front of a twenty-foot giant that looked like it weighed a ton given the closely placed branches. It was the Monday after Thanksgiving, and Mom, Donovan, Mac, Ty, Trevor, and I had all bundled up and come into the woods to cut down several trees for the house. It had been such an awesome weekend. All the people I loved most in the world had been together under the same roof for several days. Well, mostly together. Donovan did go back to the inn where he was staying each evening, but he returned each morning, and after that first night, Trevor had returned home each evening as well. I'd been tempted to join him, but ever cautious Amanda couldn't quite relax to the point of giving in to my hormones.

"It looks like Sunny found a pretty great tree for the living room," Mac added. It was true that Sunny was digging frantically at the roots of a much smaller but equally full tree.

"I'll grab the saw," Trevor said.

"And I'll grab the netting," Ty added.

The plan was to cut down the tree and then wrap it in netting for the drive home to protect the branches from flopping around in the back of Trevor's truck.

I couldn't help but smile as Mom wrapped her hand around Donovan's and then drug him off to look for pinecones to use to make the wreaths she'd been talking about for two days. I realized that a relationship between the two of them would work out just fine if they were both inclined to pursue the attraction they seemed to feel for one another. They both lived in New York and liked to travel, and Donovan had mentioned to me that he was looking to cut back his hours as he prepared for his eventual retirement. I'd been devastated when my dad had elected to keep his old life and not to go into witness protection with Mom and me, but now that I looked at the situation with adult eyes, I could see that Mom and Dad were never really suited the way Mom and Donovan seemed to be.

Donovan was great. In addition to the fact that he was one of the people in the world I could depend upon, he was also handy to have around when what seemed to be a typical local murder investigation turned international. Not only had Donald Ferguson been officially charged with playing a role in Bryson Teller's murder, but the deeper Donovan's men dug, the more widespread Ferguson's dirty dealings appeared to be. I was happy to hand things off to

Donovan's men, and I think Woody was happy to have it off his plate as well. Of course, now that we knew that a hired gun had killed Bryson and Ben Bellingham had shot Trinity, I had to wonder who'd been watching the house since I was pretty sure it wasn't either of these individuals.

That was tomorrow's problem. Ty was going home tomorrow, and while I knew Mac would miss him, she didn't seem at all inclined to go with him. They talked about the weekend, but I had the sense that, as Trevor had indicated, Mac wasn't ready to jump into anything too complicated. I was happy Mac had found Ty, but I was also happy that I wasn't losing my roommate. I was really looking forward to Mac, Trevor, and me being together this Christmas. Mom planned to stay through the new year, but I swear I overheard her and Donovan discussing the holiday dinner in such a way as to make it sound as if he might be coming back. I hoped so. The last thing I wanted to do was get in the middle of whatever was going on between him and my mom, but I really did like having him around.

"I'm going to get a small tree for my bedroom, and your mom wants one as well. Do you want one?" Mac asked.

"I do," I answered. "There is a perfect place for it in the corner near the fireplace as long as it is fairly narrow."

"Maybe we should have brought two trucks," Trevor said.

"We can just stack them and tie them down," I answered.

"I'm looking forward to decorating them," Mom smiled in such a way as to bring warmth to my heart.

"Of course, that tall one will take some work. I volunteered to help with the Christmas Carnival, so it is a good thing we are getting an early start." Mom ran her hand over the branches of one of the trees to check for freshness. "By the way, I signed you kids up to help with the carnival as well. I hope that's okay."

"I'm game," I answered.

"Me too," Mac said.

"And you know I'll help," Trevor added, "but I do have a business to run."

"I think the schedule can be pretty flexible," Mom answered. "I thought it would be fun if Tucker was Santa's reindeer again this year, so I signed you all up for shifts in the Santa House."

I groaned. "Please tell me you didn't sign me up to be an elf."

"Of course, I did, dear. You were such a cute elf the last time."

"I was sixteen."

"You look just the same to me."

I glanced at Trevor. He laughed. "I think Amanda will be an adorable elf," he added.

"Good because I have you signed up to play Santa on your days off." Mom clapped her hands together in front of her chest. "I'm just so excited. Things this year are going to be just like they used to be."

"Without the murder, kidnapping, and conspiracy," I added. Even as I said those words, I knew deep down inside that knowing my luck, murder, kidnapping, and conspiracy would be exactly the sort of thing I had to look forward to.

Up Next from Kathi Daley Books

Preview: The Mystery Before Christmas

"He moves softly through the night, unseen and unheard, leaving gifts for those in need, while the residents of snowy Foxtail Lake slumber beneath blankets piled high to ward off the chill of a Rocky Mountain winter." I turned and looked at the cat I'd been reading aloud to. "What do you think? Too flowery?"

"Meow."

"Yeah, maybe I should back off the descriptors a bit. It's just that I want to grab my readers right from the beginning. Maybe I should just say something like: 'Secret Santa strikes again,' and then talk about the latest gifts." I paused to consider this. "Honestly, most of the gifts have been delivered by means other than late-night drop-offs, but the imagery of Santa lurking around in the middle of the night is a lot more appealing than the imagery created by a wheelchair being delivered by UPS." I glanced out the window at the falling snow. The little room at the top of the house felt cozy and warm, and it was this feeling I wanted to bring to my readers. I glanced down at my laptop and began to simultaneously type and speak once again. "Not only has the mysterious gift giver, known only as Secret Santa, been busy doling out random acts of kindness to the town's residents, but he also seems to understand exactly what each gift recipient needs. Billy Prescott received a new wheelchair after his mother backed over his old one; Connie Denton was gifted a down payment on the diner where she'd worked for over twenty years that she hoped to buy from her boss when he decided to move off the mountain; Gilda Frederickson found a gift card for a winter's worth of snow shoveling services in her purse after word got out that she'd broken her hip; and Donnie Dingman walked out onto his drive to find a used four-wheel-drive vehicle so he could get to his doctor's appointments even when it snowed. Some are calling this anonymous gift giver an angel come to earth during this holiest of seasons, while others are certain the late-night Samaritan actually is Santa Clause himself." I looked at the cat. "Better?"

The cat jumped down off the desk where he'd been sitting and watching me work, and headed toward the attic window, which was cheerily draped with white twinkle lights. Apparently, my honorary editor was done listening to my drivel for the day. I supposed I didn't blame him. It did seem like I was trying too hard to find the perfect words to describe the phenomenon that had gripped my small town for the past two weeks.

I got up from the desk and joined the cat on the window seat. It felt magical to sit in the window overlooking the frozen lake as fresh snow covered the winter landscape. Great-aunt Gracie had strung colorful lights on one of the fir trees in the yard, bringing the feel of the season to the frozen landscape. Combined with the white lights draped over every shrub outdoors, and the white lights I'd strung around the window and along the ceiling of the attic, it felt like I was working in a magical fairyland.

"Maybe instead of a whimsical piece filled with artful words, I should do more of a hard-hitting expose," I suggested to the cat. "Everyone knows about the mystery person who has been gifting the citizens of Foxtail Lake with the exact gifts they most need, but no one knows who he is. Maybe I, Calliope Rose Collins, should work to unmask the Good Samaritan. I know the people he has helped with his good deeds would welcome the chance to thank him. He really is changing lives. He deserves recognition for that."

"Meow." The cat began to purr loudly as he crawled into my lap. I gently stroked his head as I considered the past two months and the changes I'd seen in my own life.

Two months ago, I'd come back to Foxtail Lake after a terrible accident had shattered my world. At the time, I was a broken woman simply looking for somewhere to lick my wounds, but in the two months I'd been here, not only had I finally begun to accept my new situation, but I'd made quite a few strides in my effort to reinvent my life as well. While my years as a concert pianist would always hold a special place in my heart, I loved volunteering at the Foxtail Lake Animal Shelter, and I adored my new career as a columnist for the local newspaper, a role I'd earned after I'd helped my childhood friend, Cass Wylander, solve not only a present-day murder but the twenty-year-old murder of my best friend Stella Steinmetz as well. After the case was solved, I wrote about my experience, the local newspaper picked it up, and as they say, the rest is history. The article was so well received that I'd been offered a weekly column to fill with whatever subject matter I chose.

Unfolding myself from the window, I crossed the room and sat back down at the old desk that I'd shoved into the center of the attic to use as my temporary office. The article on Secret Santa would be the fourth article I'd written for the newspaper. The first article on Stella's murder had been published in mid-November, followed by an article about the missing dogs from the animal shelter where I volunteered, and then an investigative piece relating to the controversy surrounding the misappropriation of the funds which should have been earmarked to pay for the annual tree lighting. The stories I wrote weren't the hard-hitting exposes a real investigative reporter might pen, but I had helped Cass find Stella's killer, I had found the missing dogs and the man who took them, and I had found the cleverly disguised missing money after it was announced the annual tree lighting would be canceled.

Of course, I'd had Cass to help out with Stella's murder and the missing dogs. He would probably have been happy to help with the missing funds as well, but that story broke right about the same time Buford Norris turned up dead. Buford was an ornery sort who tended to drink too much, so after his body was found buried beneath the snow, most people just assumed he'd passed out and froze to death. But Cass wasn't quite as sure as some of the other town folk were that Buford had passed out on his own. Investigating the man's death as possible foul play wasn't sitting well with the sheriff or the mayor, but Cass was a conscientious sort who wasn't going to close a case based on a maybe.

"Is Paisley coming for a piano lesson today?" Great-aunt Gracie called up the stairs.

"She is," I called back down the stairs of the large lakefront home I'd grown up in. "Anna has dance after school, so her mother can't give Paisley a ride home. I was planning to pick her up."

"I'm going to run to the market. I can pick her up if you'd like."

"That'd be great."

Paisley Holloway was our ten-year-old neighbor who was living with her grandmother after her mother passed just before Thanksgiving. Gracie and I were doing what we could to help out since the grandmother had her own health issues to deal with. Most days, Paisley got a ride to and from school with her friend, Anna, but on the days Anna's mother was unable to provide a ride, Gracie or I picked her up from school. On the days we picked her up, we usually brought her here to the house, helped her with her homework, and generally did what we could to make things easier for everyone involved. It really was a terrible situation. One that no ten-year-old should have to live through. I'd lost my parents when I was young as well, so I knew better than most how important it was to have a safe harbor in the storm.

"Is Alastair up there with you?" Aunt Gracie called after a few minutes had passed.

I looked at the longhaired black cat who'd jumped back onto the desk next to me. "He is."

"Okay, make sure he doesn't get out. There is a storm blowing in, and I wouldn't want him to get trapped out in it."

"I'll keep an eye on him," I called. I supposed I should have gotten up and headed downstairs when

Gracie first called up since it would have cut down on all the yelling back and forth. "Just send Paisley up when you get back. Alastair and I are working on this week's column."

"Okay. If you see Tom, let him know that dinner will be at six tonight."

Tom Walden was Gracie's groundskeeper, although, in reality, he was so much more. He'd lived on the property with Gracie for more than forty years. Tom and Gracie were friends, good friends who shared their lives. Sometimes I wondered if they weren't something more.

Once Gracie left, I returned my attention to the blank page in front of me. I had to admit the idea of a Secret Santa intrigued me. Not only because this particular Santa had already spent tens of thousands of dollars gifting deserving citizens with items they needed but would unable to buy on their own, but also because he'd been doing it for almost two weeks and so far no one had figured out who he was. There were theories, of course. A lot of them. Based on the monetary value of the gifts, it seemed pretty obvious the Secret Santa was someone of means. Though our town was small, and those who'd lived here for a lifetime tended not to be the sort to acquire a large amount of wealth, the town did tend to attract more than its share of retirees, many of whom were quite wealthy when they arrived. Since I was suddenly determined to identify Secret Santa in my column, I started a list of possible 'suspects' after taking the monetary outlay into consideration.

The first name to come to mind was Carolyn Worthington. Carolyn was an heiress who'd lived in Boston until two years ago when her only child, a son in his forties, had died in an accident. Shattered to her core, she realized she needed a complete change, so she bought an estate on the east shore of the lake and then quickly made friends by volunteering in the community. Carolyn was quick to share her wealth and had given a lot of money away in the past, which made her both a good and a poor candidate for Secret Santa. If Carolyn was doing the good deeds then why the sudden secrecy? Still, given her wealth and her altruistic nature, she was on the top of most of the suspect lists in town.

And then there was Haviland Hargrove, a lifelong Foxtail Lake resident, whose grandfather had struck it rich during the gold rush of the nineteenth century. Haviland wasn't as naturally altruistic as Carolyn, but he certainly had the means to buy everything that had been purchased and then some. He was a man in his eighties who'd had a few health problems, so perhaps he'd decided to spread his wealth around a bit before he passed on.

Dean and Martin Simpson were brothers who'd made a fortune in the software industry. The men lived together in a mansion set in the center of a gated estate. Neither had ever married nor had children and while they didn't go out and socialize a lot, they were pleasant enough and had several good friends in the community, including my friend, Cass, who played poker with them twice a month. Cass didn't think that Dean and Martin were our Secret Santa's, but I wasn't so sure about that.

There were a handful of other locals with the means to do what was being done. I supposed that once I developed my list, I'd just start interviewing folks. Someone must know something that would point me in the right direction. I supposed there were those who felt I should leave well enough alone, and perhaps they were right, but after stumbling across a really juicy mystery like this one, anyone who knew me knew I was prone to follow the clues to the end.

"Anyone home?" Tom called.

I got up and walked to the top of the stairs. "I'm here. Aunt Gracie went to the market. She said to tell you that dinner will be at six."

"That should work. Did she happen to say what she wanted me to do with the tree ornaments she had me pick up while I was in Lakewood?"

I decided to head down the stairs rather than continuing this conversation as a yelling match. "She didn't say. I'm surprised she wanted additional ornaments. We have boxes of them in the attic."

"I guess these are special. Custom made. I'll just leave them on the dining table for now."

I glanced out the open door at the darkening sky, mindful of Gracie's warning about not letting Alastair out. "I'm sure that is fine. Let me lock the cat in the den, and I'll help you carry everything in."

"I'd appreciate that. It seems your aunt has gone decorating crazy this year."

I looked around the house, which was already decked out with garland, candles, wreaths, and bright red bows. She really had outdone herself. When I'd asked her about it, she'd mumbled something about wanting the place to be cheerful for Paisley, but truth be told, I think she was just happy to have others in the house to celebrate with this year.

"As far as you know, are we still getting the tree this week?" I asked Tom after we headed out into the frigid afternoon.

"As far as I know. If this storm dumps as much snow as it is calling for, then I'm afraid her plan to go into the forest to cut a tree might have to be altered. Walter has some nice ones on his lot. I took a look while I was there to pick up the branches Gracie wanted for the mantle."

"I would think a tree from Walter's lot would be just fine. If we can cut one, we will, but if not, we'll work together to sell Gracie on the tree lot idea." I picked up the first of the five boxes in the back of Tom's truck. "I'm really happy she is enjoying the holiday so much this year, but I'm afraid she is going to overdo. Not only has she gone crazy decorating but she signed up to be the co-chair for the Christmas in the Mountains event as well."

"Your aunt has a lot of energy. I'm sure she'll be fine. We just need to be sure to help out as much as we can."

"I guess."

"Gracie wants you to have the perfect Christmas. Like the ones the two of you shared when you were younger. This is important to her."

I glanced up at the sky filled with snow flurries as I started toward the house. "It's important to me as well, and I do plan to help out as much as I can. Of course, researching Secret Santa is going to keep me busy. I think I've pretty much decided to focus on figuring out who Secret Santa is rather than the gifts he has delivered. You haven't heard anything have you?"

Tom set his box on the table next to mine, and we both turned around to go for the next load.

"Everyone seems to have an opinion, but I haven't heard that anyone has come up with any proof as to the identity of Secret Santa if that is what you are asking. The guys down at the lodge think it might be Fisher."

I raised a brow. "Ford Fisher? Why do the guys think it's him? As far as I know, the man isn't rich." Ford Fisher used to own one of the pubs in town before it sold, so I imagined he'd done okay in terms of saving for retirement, but I doubted he had tens of thousands of dollars to give away.

"I think Ford might have more stashed away than one might think. There is a lot of money in alcohol, and Ford has lived simply for much of his life. In my mind, he doesn't have the right temperament to be a Secret Santa, but he has been acting oddly lately, which is why I think the guys at the lodge suspect him."

I headed back to the house with the second load of boxes. "Acting oddly, how?" I wondered.

"Secretive. Evasive. He hasn't shown up at the lodge in three weeks, and when some of the guys went by his place to see if he was okay, he told them he was fine but didn't even invite them in. I've called him several times, even left messages, but he hasn't called me back."

"Sounds like he might be depressed. Do you know if he suffers from depression?" I set my box next to the others on the table.

"Not that I know of. Ford's always been a real social sort. Other than those few times when he was too hungover to make it to the lodge, he's pretty much been there every Wednesday and Friday since I've been going. Not that I go every week. Sometimes Gracie and I do something, but Ford is a real regular."

"It sounds like you and your friends might be right to be worried about him. I'd continue to check on him if he doesn't start coming around. Having said that, in my mind, his overall mood doesn't seem to have a Secret Santa feel."

Tom headed back out of the final box. I tagged along after him in spite of the fact there was just one box left to fetch.

"Yeah," Tom agreed. "The idea of him being Secret Santa doesn't sit quite right with me either. I hope he isn't ill. He didn't say he was feeling poorly, but that could explain his absences."

"Wasn't Ford friends with Buford?" I asked. "Maybe he is just missing the guy."

"Maybe," Tom agreed. "Ford and Buford went at it like two old dogs with a thorn in their paws most of the time, but in the end, I guess you could say they were friends. I don't suppose Cass has proven one way or another what happened to Buford?"

I shook my head. "On the one hand, Buford had been drinking on the night he died and could very well have wandered out into the blizzard, passed out, and froze to death. On the other hand, Buford had a bump on his head that looked as if it had been inflicted by someone hitting him with a heavy object."

"Could he have hit his head when he passed out?" Tom asked.

"He could have, but the position his body was found in and the location of the bump doesn't tend to support that theory. Of course, Buford could have bumped his head earlier in the day and the fact that he had a knot the size of a jawbreaker doesn't necessarily mean that injury was enough to cause him to fall to the ground in a state of unconsciousness. At this point, Cass is following the idea that Buford was hit on the head, blacked out, and then froze to death. I guess we'll just have to wait to see where his investigation ends up. I'm sure if Buford simply passed out on account of all the alcohol he drank, that scenario will float to the surface at some point." I looked up as the sound of a car approaching permeated the still air. "That must be Gracie. Paisley will be with her. Maybe we can talk about this some more over dinner."

"That'd be fine. The truth as to what happened to Buford has been weighing on my mind. It'd be nice to know one way or the other."

Yes, I agreed. It would be nice to know for certain what had caused a man who'd lived here for most of his life to simply perish in an early but not all that spectacular storm. I knew the mayor was pushing the idea that Buford's death was nothing more than a terrible accident. I supposed I didn't blame him. The town was just beginning to recover from the murder of twelve-year-old Tracy Porter. If it was determined that Buford had been murdered as well, it would most definitely bring back the fear and paranoia that had permeated the town after Tracy's death. Cass wasn't the sort to simply grasp onto the easy answer; he was the sort to want nothing short of the truth. Sometimes I wondered if his dogged commitment to following his instincts rather than the dictate of his boss wasn't going to get him fired. I supposed that it was more important to Cass to be true to his convictions than it was to keep the job he seemed to do better than anyone else did. I supposed I really admired him for that. In fact, the more I got to know Deputy Cass

Wylander, the more convinced I was that my childhood friend had grown into a man I could not only respect but grow to love if I was interested in something like that, which I wasn't.

Books by Kathi Daley

Come for the murder, stay for the romance

Zoe Donovan Cozy Mystery:

Halloween Hijinks
The Trouble With Turkeys
Christmas Crazy
Cupid's Curse
Big Bunny Bump-off
Beach Blanket Barbie
Maui Madness
Derby Divas
Haunted Hamlet
Turkeys, Tuxes, and Tabbies
Christmas Cozy
Alaskan Alliance
Matrimony Meltdown
Soul Surrender
Heavenly Honeymoon
Hopscotch Homicide
Ghostly Graveyard
Santa Sleuth
Shamrock Shenanigans
Kitten Kaboodle
Costume Catastrophe
Candy Cane Caper
Holiday Hangover
Easter Escapade
Camp Carter
Trick or Treason
Reindeer Roundup
Hippity Hoppity Homicide

Firework Fiasco
Henderson House
Holiday Hostage
Lunacy Lake
Celtic Christmas – *December 2019*

Zimmerman Academy The New Normal
Zimmerman Academy New Beginnings
Ashton Falls Cozy Cookbook

Tj Jensen Paradise Lake Mystery:
Pumpkins in Paradise
Snowmen in Paradise
Bikinis in Paradise
Christmas in Paradise
Puppies in Paradise
Halloween in Paradise
Treasure in Paradise
Fireworks in Paradise
Beaches in Paradise
Thanksgiving in Paradise

Whales and Tails Cozy Mystery:
Romeow and Juliet
The Mad Catter
Grimm's Furry Tail
Much Ado About Felines
Legend of Tabby Hollow
Cat of Christmas Past
A Tale of Two Tabbies
The Great Catsby
Count Catula
The Cat of Christmas Present

A Winter's Tail
The Taming of the Tabby
Frankencat
The Cat of Christmas Future
Farewell to Felines
A Whisker in Time
The Catsgiving Feast
A Whale of a Tail
The Catnap Before Christmas

Writers' Retreat Mystery:
First Case
Second Look
Third Strike
Fourth Victim
Fifth Night
Sixth Cabin
Seventh Chapter
Eighth Witness
Ninth Grave

Rescue Alaska Mystery:
Finding Justice
Finding Answers
Finding Courage
Finding Christmas
Finding Shelter – *Early 2020*

A Tess and Tilly Mystery:
The Christmas Letter
The Valentine Mystery
The Mother's Day Mishap
The Halloween House

The Thanksgiving Trip
The Saint Paddy's Promise
The Halloween Haunting
The Christmas Clause – *November 2019*

The Inn at Holiday Bay:
Boxes in the Basement
Letters in the Library
Message in the Mantel
Answers in the Attic
Haunting in the Hallway
Pilgrim in the Parlor
Note in the Nutcracker – *December 2019*

A Cat in the Attic Mystery:
The Curse of Hollister House
The Mystery before Christmas - *November 2019*

The Hathaway Sisters:
Harper
Harlow
Hayden – *Early 2020*

Haunting by the Sea:
Homecoming by the Sea
Secrets by the Sea
Missing by the Sea
Betrayal by the Sea
Thanksgiving by the Sea

Sand and Sea Hawaiian Mystery:
Murder at Dolphin Bay

Murder at Sunrise Beach
Murder at the Witching Hour
Murder at Christmas
Murder at Turtle Cove
Murder at Water's Edge
Murder at Midnight
Murder at Pope Investigations

Seacliff High Mystery:
The Secret
The Curse
The Relic
The Conspiracy
The Grudge
The Shadow
The Haunting

Road to Christmas Romance:
Road to Christmas Past

USA Today best-selling author Kathi Daley lives in beautiful Lake Tahoe with her husband Ken. When she isn't writing, she likes spending time hiking the miles of desolate trails surrounding her home. She has authored more than a hundred books in eleven series, including Zoe Donovan Cozy Mysteries, Whales and Tails Island Mysteries, Tess and Tilly Cozy Mysteries, Sand and Sea Hawaiian Mysteries, Tj Jensen Paradise Lake Series, Inn at Holiday Bay Cozy Mysteries, Writers' Retreat Southern Seashore Mysteries, Rescue Alaska Paranormal Mysteries, Haunting by the Sea Paranormal Mysteries, Family Ties Mystery Romances, and Seacliff High Teen Mysteries. Find out more about her books at www.kathidaley.com

Stay up-to-date:
Newsletter, *The Daley Weekly* http://eepurl.com/NRPDf
Webpage – www.kathidaley.com
Facebook at Kathi Daley Books –
www.facebook.com/kathidaleybooks
Kathi Daley Books Group Page –
https://www.facebook.com/groups/569578823146850/
E-mail – kathidaley@kathidaley.com
Twitter at Kathi Daley@kathidaley –
https://twitter.com/kathidaley
Amazon Author Page –
https://www.amazon.com/author/kathidaley
BookBub – https://www.bookbub.com/authors/kathi-daley

55985071R00116